BOOK THREE OF THE GALLAGHER GIRLS MYSTERIES

GAIL GRANT PARK

A
HAUNTING
AT
HAWTHORN

and other ghostly tales

For more information, address: gail@gailgrantpark.com or visit http://gailgrantpark.com

Paperback ISBN: 979-8-9919679-0-7
Hardcover ISBN: 979-8-9919679-1-4

Cover design by Patrick Knowles

For all my ancestors.
Their stories have shaped me and provided the
inspiration for these tales

Table of Contents

A Haunting at Hawthorn

And Other Ghostly Tales

Irish Vocabulary

Book One: A Haunting at Hawthorn

Oíche mhaith leat = ee-ha wah lat = good night used formally

Spaiaí go leor = spah-tee guh lyor = plenty of space. Light-hearted way to say goodnight

Press = cupboard

Sionainn = Shannon

Farls = soft, buttery, flatbread made from cooked potato

A mhuirnín = A vwer-neen = sweetheart, darling

Cailín babby = girl child

Knacker = obnoxious ruffian, lowlife

Croía = KREE-ya = heart

Mo chroi = mo kree = my heart

Eamon = AY-muhn

Mairéad = **MAW-rade** = Irish form of Margaret = "pearl."

Bronagh = BRO-nah = sorrow

Mhuireann = Mwir-eann

Cathaoirleach = Ka-hear-loh = chair of the city council

Clodagh = CLO-dah

Eoin = OH-in

C'mere to me = listen, I need to tell you something important

G'way = seriously?

Anna Livia = traditional name given to the River Liffey, honouring the river goddess, Lífe

Codding = joking

Deadly = great

Slán go foill, mo stór = slawn guh foil muh store = goodbye for now, my love

Book Two: Death Down Under

Síofra = SHEE-fra

Clíódhna = KLEE-na = Queen of the Banshees

Danu = Da-NEW = Mother Goddess

Conas atá tú? = How are you?

Maimeó = MAH-mo = grandmother

Whānau = Māori for family

Book Three: Buried Secrets

Mo chroi = muh khree = my heart

Tabhair aire = TOR- ara = take care of yourself

Go raibh maith agat = Guh-rev-may-agut = thank you

Dia dhuit = dee-ah-gwit = hello

Dia is Muire dhuit = jee-ah-iss-mwir-a-gwit = response to hello

Bubble and squeak = fried leftovers, mostly potatoes, meat and vegetables, traditionally carrots and cabbage.

A leanbh = uh LAN-uv = my child, a term of endearment

Seanmháthair = SHEN a var = grandmother

Gliondar mo chroí = delight of my heart

Scut work = dirty work, hard manual labour

bogging = dirty

Geebag = someone intensely disliked

Go n-éirí leat = Guh n-eye-ree lat = Goodbye and good luck

Fachtna = FACHT na = Irish saint. The name means malicious, hostile

Richael = REE – chul = purity, devotion = Irish patron saint of ewes, lambs

Róisín = Row-SHEEN = little rose

Gowls = someone you dislike

Book Four: Gone But Not Forgotten

Athbhliain faoi mhaise dhuit = Af vlian fe vasha gwit = Happy New Year

Aoibh = EE-va

Niamh = NEE-iv

Bail ó Dhia ort = Bahl oh yee-uh ort = God bless you (a greeting)

Craic was ninety = very fun

Splitting the stones = a sunny day

Delirah = delighted

Scarlet = embarrassed

Caoimhe = KEE-va

Fluthered = drunk

Dosser = someone that's doing anything other than what they should be doing

Gráinne = GRON-ya

Book Five: Bad Blood

Italian translations:

Cuore mio = my heart

La mia ragazza = my girlfriend

Il mio consigliere e il mio consigliere e compagno = my advisor and companion

Così felice = so happy

Cara mia = My dear

Meravigliosa = wonderful, marvellous

Piacere = nice to meet you

Grazie = thank you

bella giornata = beautiful day

Luce dei miei occhi, = light of my eyes

Una piccola bugia = a small fib

Per l'amor del Cielo = for heaven's sake

Ti voglio bene, fratello = I wish you well, brother

la sua fidanzata = his girlfriend

Una piccola bugia bianca = a little white lie

La famiglia continua = the family goes on

Slán a fhágáil agat agus tú a fheiceáil go luath = slan all gall agut agus tua ecall ga lua = Goodbye and see you soon

Author's note on spelling

As this book takes place in Ireland and the main characters are Irish, I use the version of English that is standard there. Thus, you'll find colour but not color, recognise, but not recognize, etc. I am sure my American readers can easily surmount this challenge and hope it will provide a feeling of accomplishment as you come to easily cruise over the unfamiliar spellings.

A Haunting at Hawthorn

Chapter I

—

Is maith an scáthán súil charad
A friend's eye is a good mirror.

—Irish Proverb

Kildare, Spring 2012

"There's a locked door on the second floor that's stuck. None of the keys you gave me seem to work."

Nuala turned from the starters she was prepping to address Siobhán, her newly hired, part-time house cleaner. "Locked or stuck?"

"The doorknob turns but I can't pull it open."

"Okay, give me a minute to search for Sean's keyring — I don't think he took it with him to the auction — wait, you know what? Don't worry about it. I'll figure it out before your next visit. Just skip that room for now."

"Sounds good. I'll be another thirty minutes or so then."

"Thanks, Siobhán. I couldn't begin to do all the cleaning in this place on my own."

With Seán gone overnight to the horse auction, it wasn't until later that evening when Nuala returned from the catering gig that she remembered the locked room. Still fuelled by adrenaline after the success of the party, she couldn't settle into sleep and determined to look at the locked door.

She located Seán's ring of keys in his top right desk drawer and armed with those, plus her own household set of keys, she bounded up the stairs to the second floor. With the master suite on the main floor, she rarely came up here, as she and Seán had a hard enough time finding uses for all the rooms below. This upper area had been mainly used as guest rooms and servants' quarters, something they had no use for.

It didn't take her long to ascertain which room Siobhán had referred to, as she had left all the other doors open, and the windows cracked to let in the fresh spring air and dispel the cloying smell of dust and disuse. Several keys on Seán's ring fitted the lock but wouldn't turn. She finally found one that turned slightly, but then stopped short of disengaging the lock.

Nuala removed the key and got down on her knees to peer into the lock. She brushed a wayward strand of her chestnut pageboy away from her eyes and shown the torch into the opening. There was something white — a piece of paper? — wedged into the hole. Running down to her bedroom, she grabbed her tweezers from the bath and made her way back to the locked room.

It took some time to finesse the paper free, but when it finally came loose, she saw that it had been folded several times into a tiny square. She carefully unfolded it, but the paper was blank.

Hmm. What is that all about?

Nuala tucked the tiny wad into her pocket then tried the key again. The faint click told her it was disengaged. She turned the handle and pushed. The room was sparsely furnished as a bedchamber with a twin-sized iron-frame bedstead, devoid of mattress. Next to the bed was a wooden cradle. As Nuala entered the room, a tingle shot up her spine and her heart began to beat faster. Something about that cradle was drawing her in.

Peering into the small space, she couldn't explain the dread she felt. What did she expect to find, a tiny skeleton? Her imagination was running away from her. The cradle was empty. She breathed out heavily, but the dread remained. *Why had the room been locked? Why was the lock jammed? Who had stayed here?*

The euphoria from the successful catering event had

dissipated and she suddenly felt drained and exhausted. For some reason unknown to even herself, she locked the door once again behind her. But as she removed the key and dropped it into her pocket, she felt a breeze blow through the hall, and in the breeze, the whispered words *find my baby* wafted softly into her mind.

Sean wouldn't be home until late the next evening, but Nuala had to talk to someone. Who else but her sister, Moira, who had been hearing ghostly whispers since she was a wean. It was going on half-eleven — too late to call? Nuala texted first:

—You awake?

A few minutes later, the response:

—What's up?

—Want to talk?

—Please!

Her mobile buzzed: Moira. With no preamble or greeting, Nuala blurted: "I think I just heard my first Visitor from Beyond."

Chapter 2

*'Tis baois a bheith críonna san áit a bhfuil an
t-aineolas bliss.*
'Tis a folly to be wise where ignorance is bliss.

—Irish Proverb

After recounting the tale to her sister, Nuala asked, "What can it mean?"

"It doesn't make sense," Moira replied. "Remember when we searched the whole place last year looking for what turned out to be Patrick Mahoney's ghost? We went through all the rooms on that upper floor and there was nothing unusual at that time."

"I know, I know. And before we were married and moved in, Seán had the whole place deep cleaned. I don't even remember seeing the cradle up there, let alone the stuck door."

"Someone is messing with you."

"How can that be? And why?"

"I can't answer that. Will you be okay there on your own for the night?"

"I'll be grand. It's late. Try to get some sleep."

"Call me in the morning?"

"I will," Nuala promised. "Oíche mhaith leat."

"Spataí go leor," Moira replied.

Nuala laughed, "Thanks, I'll need it — 'space' from haunting spirits, that is!"

After tossing and turning for some time, Nuala was finally able to sleep, but dreams continued to disturb her rest. In one dream, she was exploring the house and entered the attic where there remained items from the previous owners — paintings, old furniture, boxes of who-knows-what. In one box she pulled out a quilt. It was quite old, moth-eaten and fragile, but she could make out the pattern of blocks that made up the quilt. It looked like a hawthorn tree that was embroidered with family names. Branches led off in aberrant directions. Horses lined the perimeter, prancing around the edgework. Along one of the side branches was a hole eaten through by mice (she could see their droppings on the floor around the box). She was filled with a feeling of anxiety to know whose name had been obliterated by the mice's handiwork. As she looked around, she saw tufts of cloth, scraps of the fabric from the quilt. She frantically tried to gather up the pieces and fit them together to discover if they were part of the missing section. Then she woke up.

She checked the time: five o'clock. She needed to get up anyway and feed the horses. Connor, their stud manager, didn't arrive until nine o'clock each morning and the horses couldn't wait that long for their oats.

As Nuala dished out their breakfast and refilled the water buckets, she talked softly to each one. They each nuzzled her in return. She loved the feel of their velvety soft, warm muzzles on her skin. With only six horses in their stud operations, she still felt like she knew each one individually and loved them all. This was her dream — or a big part of it — to be around these noble, graceful, and majestic beings.

After finishing up in the stables, Nuala returned to the kitchen and prepared her own breakfast. It was close to half-eight when her mobile chirped: Moira.

"Howya?"

"It's me. What's the craic? Any more visitors during the night?"

"I had a dream, if that counts," Nuala reported.

"With you it does," Moira replied. "Tell me."

After recounting the attic visit and the quilt, Nuala added, "I felt compelled to check when it was light and there is no quilt in a box, or any other indicators of my dream in the actual attic."

"Well, sure and I wouldn't expect there to be. But it seems like a clue that the quilt indicated family history information. Certainly not your own, as you have no ties to the house prior to your marriage to Seán. It's more likely that it belongs to your mystery visitor."

"That's what I was thinking. Not sure how I'd go about learning more concerning the prior inhabitants, though, apart from who's in the family cemetery and what I already unearthed in the records about the line of inheritance for the estate."

"That's your and Ma's area of expertise; sorry I can't help you there."

"But you do know about inviting Others to visit. I'd love to hear more from the Whisperer of last night."

"Do you want me to come by and check it out?" Moira asked, a hint of hope in her voice.

"Maybe. If you're free this weekend, you and Deirdre could come by for Sunday brunch. I'm dying to try out a few recipe ideas and you would make perfect guinea pigs. Seán will be home this evening. I want to talk to him about it and see if he is aware of any peculiarities in the McGuire family that he hasn't told me about yet. Since they have been the sole owners of the property prior to Seán, it's got to be another one of their doings. As you know, it wouldn't be the first time they've been the catalyst for unsettling spirits."

"Right. Okay then, I'll catch you later. Bye-bye!"

"Byebyebye. Bye —, hey, wait! You could do one thing for me."

"Sure, and I will. What is it?"

"Hawthorn trees. I'd swear the image on the quilt was a hawthorn. Ask Deirdre what the symbolism and mythology of the hawthorn is. I know about it being tied to and protected by the fairies and all, but maybe there's more I should know."

"It came up a bit in Celtic Civ at uni. I'll pull out my notes as well."

"Okay, love you, bye-bye; bye-bye!"

"Love you, bye-bye!"

After hanging up, Nuala took a walk through the estate grounds. She loved this time of early morning when the air was crisp and clean, the birdsong loud and boisterous as the feathered community welcomed a new day. She found herself at the family cemetery and wandered among the stones. She and Seán, with the help of family and friends, had cleaned up the site, weeding and planting perennials among the markers. They had carefully removed the lichen and moss from the engravings so that they were almost all decipherable. She hadn't scrutinized them before, but now she searched the memorials for clues as to who might have visited her last night.

Patrick Mahoney's stone stood out, as it was newly installed last year at the conclusion of one of their Gallagher Investigations cases. She could put him in the 'case closed' file. The oldest tombstone was that of Philip McGuire, born 1800, died 1868. He was the first owner of the land and the one who had built the house in 1844. Next to him was his wife, Doireann.

Doireann was a potential candidate for a haunting, as Patrick's spirit had informed Moira that he had personally known of occasions when Philip had locked his own wife and sons at various times in the tower room as punishment. That would certainly warrant being an 'unsettled spirit,' Nuala mused. But Doireann's children were laid to rest right next to her in the cemetery: Marcus, who had inherited the estate from his father in 1868, and his younger brother, Broderick, who had befriended Patrick, or Paddy, as he was referred to.

Marcus, now … Nuala knew, also from Paddy, that Marcus was a bad one. Like his abusive father, he tormented

Paddy and was party to his murder. What was his sad domestic tale? 'Hannah, wife of Marcus' was buried near her two children who died in infancy: Caroline in 1857 and Liam in 1859. Hannah, it would seem, died in childbirth shortly after her infant son. She had given birth to a son, Hugh, in 1855, and it was Hugh who inherited the estate in 1905. It must have been a lonely childhood for Hugh, growing up as an only surviving child without a mother, and on top of that, to have had Marcus for his father. Did bad blood run in the family?

Nuala continued to inspect each stone, stopping to ponder, hoping for inspiration. It would appear from the stones that Hugh had only one child, William, born in 1900 and died in 1985. That was a long life! But was it a good one? She found markers — no headstones — for one … two … three wives of William McGuire. The first died in 1946. Inscribed on her marker was also the words, 'and stillborn daughter, 1946.' Wife number two, also receiving only a marker flush with the earth, died in 1956. Nuala couldn't see any markers indicating children for her.

Wife number three, Oona Tully, born 1926, died 1977. *Hmm. That would put her a full 26 years younger than her husband, William.*

From her previous research into the family during the investigation to establish Seán's claim to his mother's inheritance, Nuala knew that Oona's son was John McGuire, the man who had married Seán's mother. She would have to investigate civil and parish records further to try to unscramble what it all meant. She decided to come back here with Moira and Deirdre on Sunday. Maybe they could add some insights.

Somewhat reluctantly, she left the cemetery and continued her walk. She reached the paddocks just as Connor was releasing the last stallion for grazing. The horses needed no encouragement to enter the enclosure where the new spring growth of ryegrass and clover awaited them.

Nuala whistled and her favourite, a dark bay she named 'Nutmeg,' trotted over. Of course, Nutmeg wasn't his actual name. They were all registered with long, fancy names that to Nuala, were ridiculous. She preferred the pet names she had come up with based on their colouring and her penchant for all things culinary: Nutmeg, Ginger, Cinnamon, Pepper, Coffee, and Cocoa. Nutmeg let her stroke his long, graceful neck, then turned and trotted back to his mates.

Nuala sighed, chatted briefly with Connor, then walked back to the house. She had some things to do before Seán returned that evening, one of which was to bake his favourite dessert, Irish apple cake with custard sauce.

Thanks to Siobhán's help, there wasn't much in the way of cleaning she needed to do, but there were some calls to make for her business, *From Starters to Afters*. She would check in with her partner, Molly Ronan, who was based in Schull at Dymphna Gallagher's bed and breakfast inn. There were also a couple calls to clients with upcoming events she needed to firm up.

Seán told her she didn't *need* to work; the stud farm was building up a nice clientele of its own and his inheritance from his mother more than took care of any extras they may want. *She* told *him* that yes, she certainly *did* need to work. It fed her soul, and her catering business was a passion she intended to follow. Seán understood. He'd had to come to understand a lot of things outside his comfort zone when he entwined his life with hers, not least of which was the partnership she had with her sisters, Moira and Deirdre, to assist departed spirits with the unfinished business that was tying them to this world and keeping them from moving on to the Otherside.

Chapter 3

Is milis béal ciúin a chloisteáil.
A silent mouth is sweet to hear.

—Irish Proverb

"Acushla! This was amazing! Being on the road, in hotels for the last two days, I've sorely missed your wonderful cooking. And dessert —" Seán groaned as he patted his full stomach. He pulled her to him, and she sat on his knee. "I shouldn't need to eat for the rest of the evening, but after I digest this, I may have to come back for a second piece of that apple custard cake."

Nuala gave him a quick peck on his cheek and smiled. Then she stood to clear the table.

"Here, let me help you with that," Seán said, picking up plates. Working together they got the dishes washed, dried and put in the press.

"Come here to me; I've got some things to tell you," Nuala said, taking his hand and leading him to the front room.

"Uh oh, this sounds serious," Seán said, sitting next to her on the settee and continuing to hold her hand.

"I wanted to wait until you'd had a chance to eat and unwind after your trip. It's nothing awful, but something you yourself have hinted at before. I've had an encounter with a spirit."

"Good or bad? Are you okay? Why didn't you say something right away?" Seán's agitation was evident in his voice as it rose in volume. He looked around as if to spy out the responsible party. From his own experience, he knew spirits *could* cause harm.

"I'm grand. Everything's grand. It was just a whisper — a woman asking for her baby. I was hoping you would know something about the former inhabitants that could explain such an occurrence."

Seán had jumped up and was pacing in front of her. "Where did this happen?"

"Upstairs. Shall I show you?"

They walked up the stairs and Nuala pointed out the door, still shut. Standing in front of it, Seán tried the doorknob.

"It's locked," he said, stating the obvious.

"I relocked it afterwards. Silly, I know, but …" Nuala took the key from her pocket and handed it to him. He unlocked it and they went inside. The bedstead and cradle were still there as she had left them.

"Do you remember these being here before?" Nuala asked.

"Not really, but that doesn't mean they weren't here. Not everything was sold in the estate sale. We hadn't gotten to all the rooms up here to renovate yet, so it's possible they've been here from before we moved in. If you'll remember, all these rooms were chock full of junk. The McGuires were the epitome of hoarders." Seán was always choosing the most plausible explanation.

"Do you hear anything now?" Seán asked expectantly.

"I don't think it works like that. Not that I'm an expert; that's why I've asked Moira to come here for Sunday brunch. I'm hoping she can make contact with this spirit. It must have just been the timing. I was in the right frame of mind; the house was so quiet … that was the first time I had ever been able to hear someone from the Otherside before."

"I heard a spirit in this very house, remember? Scared the wits out of me!"

"Right, that was Paddy. He'd been trying for ages to reach someone. You were here alone and were about to sell the place. I imagine Paddy tried his mightiest to reach you as a last-ditch effort."

"He certainly succeeded! And you're right. My next move was to contact your sister to intervene."

"All seems quiet at the moment. Let's leave it be for now and wait to see what Moira says," Nuala suggested.

They returned to the front room where Seán started a fire in the massive stone fireplace. "Winter may be over but this house still retains the chill in the evenings," he said, stoking the flames with kindling. "Now tell me more about what you've been doing while I've been gone."

"The farewell party at Rafferty's went well. Everyone raved over the spread, and I picked up another job from it — a cousin of Sionainn Rafferty is planning a bachelorette party and wants my services."

"Bang on! I'm so proud of you!"

"Thanks, I really appreciate your support. What about you? Tell me more about the new stallion that will be arriving shortly."

"He's a beauty! A thoroughbred named *Bonnie Mahogany, King of the Curragh*, but I'm sure you'll soon come up with something more suitable to your tastes," he teased.

"Hmm … I don't mind the name 'Mahogany,' he must be a dark bay," Nuala guessed.

"He is. He's also a bit feisty, but then, he's not for pleasure riding, so I'm not too worried about that," Seán said. "He arrives next week, so we have some time to get ready for him. Now, I don't know about you, but I'm about ready for seconds on that dessert!"

"Hooray! You're here!" Nuala ran out the front door to greet her sisters. She enveloped both in hugs and ushered them inside where Seán was waiting. His eyes lit up when he saw the sisters and a grin spread across his face.

"Thanks for coming! I'm feeling much better knowing you are here to get to the bottom of this. But first, Nuala has a feast all ready for you." He escorted them into the breakfast room where, with a flourish of his arm, he indicated the spread Nuala had prepared for their brunch.

"Bravo, Nuala! This was worth skipping breakfast for!" Deirdre exclaimed as Nuala began pointing out each delicacy: rashers as well as sausage, a heaping bowl of farls, a slow cooker of Irish oatmeal, an egg scramble with fried potatoes and green peppers, and ("for the road, if you've no more room,") a sweet apple bread.

"It's a first for the apple bread. I hope it's done enough in the center," Nuala worried.

"I'm sure it's class," Seán replied, giving her shoulder a squeeze.

They dug in with hearty appetites, complimenting a beaming Nuala at each entrée. With only a half-loaf of the apple bread remaining 'for the road,' and all the other platters emptied, everyone assisted in the clean-up.

"I don't know about anyone else, but I'm stuffed and could go for a wee dander at this point," Deirdre said.

"I was hoping to get a peek at the haunting place," Moira said. "Mind if I pass on the walk?"

"I'll show Moira the room if you want to go with Deirdre," Seán offered.

"Thanks, a mhuirnín, I believe I will!" Nuala replied.

Moira followed Seán up the stairs as Deirdre and Nuala headed out the front door. When they reached the room, Seán opened it and stepped aside for Moira to go in.

"Thanks, Seán. If you don't mind, I'd like to sit here awhile and just listen."

"Right. Do you want a chair? I can get one from another room and set it here in the hall."

"That's okay. I'll just hunker down on the floor across from the room."

"Give a yell if you need anything. I'll be just below."

Once he had gone, Moira made herself comfortable with her back up against the wall and her knees pulled up to her chest. She took a deep breath in, held it a moment, then let it out slowly. She closed her eyes and whispered, *"I'm here. I'm listening. What do you need?"*

Then she waited.

Chapter 4

Ní sheasann sac folamh.
An empty sack cannot stand.

—Irish Proverb

"It feels like ages since I've seen you to just chat. How are things? What do you hear from Giulio?" Nuala said as she locked arms with her older sister.

"The last email I got from him was over a month ago. He didn't say much, just that his Ma was doing well after her accident and broken leg and all."

"Does he say when he's coming back?" Nuala asked.

"We haven't spoken about that in some time. I think he is looking into a teaching position here and hopes his internship in the history department last year will be a boost for his resumé."

"But how do you feel about that? Are you ready to

resume your relationship in person?" Nuala pressed. "You haven't been dating much since he left …"

"I'm still not sure. I care very much about him, but I was feeling so stifled at the end before he went back to Italy. I didn't feel like he respected what we did in our business. He *is* a fine thing though … and we had a lot of good times," Deirdre said with a far-off look. She shuddered involuntarily, then changed the conversation.

"Moira said you were wanting to know about trees," Deirdre said as they walked on, approaching the family cemetery.

"Did she tell you about my dream?" Nuala asked.

"She did, but I'd rather hear it again directly from you," Deirdre replied.

After recounting her dream of the quilt in the attic, Nuala said, "I came out to the family cemetery here and took some notes on the names and dates, but I haven't been able to come up with anything plausible for the voice I heard."

They stopped for a moment at the small family cemetery for Deirdre to walk down the rows of stones and read the inscriptions.

"This William McGuire could be a possible candidate. Not himself, of course, but one of his wives. He's got three here, and reading between the lines, I'll bet he was looking for a male heir. The first wife died young — only thirty-one — after giving birth to a stillborn. The second wife died only ten years after the first. I don't see any children here for her either. That could be a suspicious death, knowing the reputation of the McGuire men we are aware of at least. The third, Oona, lived to be in her fifties, but as you've probably noticed, she was quite a bit younger than William — prime for childbearing."

"She was John's mother, and I did notice that, as well as the age differences of William's wives, but I hadn't thought it might be tied to William's desire for a male heir. That's good detecting!"

Deirdre smiled. "I could be way off base, but it's a starting place."

"I called Ma; she is going to help me on the records end. We are looking into children born within the years of William's lifespan to any of his three wives that may be unaccounted for here in the cemetery."

"That would be helpful."

"What would be helpful is if Moira can just talk to the spirit who started all this!"

Moira felt a chill breeze. She opened her eyes and glanced

at the window at the end of the hall, but it was closed. She stood up and moved towards the door to the room containing the bedstead and cradle. The cradle was rocking slightly. She entered the room, and the rocking stopped.

"I may be able to help you if you let me," Moira said softly.

"No one can help. It's too late; he already took her away from me."

"Are you able to show yourself to me? I feel at a disadvantage, as you can see me, but I can't see you."

"I can't believe you can hear me! That hasn't happened in …"

"In how long? Who are you and when did you die?"

A shimmering of the air in front of Moira coalesced into the shape of a young woman with long, dark hair. She was clothed in a white shift, barefoot, with a brown shawl wrapped around her shoulders, which she held tightly to her chest.

"My name is Mairéad Ashe and William McGuire is responsible for my death when he took my baby away from me."

"He took your baby and murdered you?" Moira repeated, seeking clarification.

"His exact words were: 'I don't need a cailín babby. You were supposed to give me a son!' He took the child, and I never saw her again. He let me stay another week or so, then said 'it was best' that I find another situation, gave me a ten-pound note and shut the door behind me."

"That knacker! How awful! What did you do?"

"I wanted to find my little one, but I didn't know where to go. He told me he found her a new home, but indicated it was far away from here and I wasn't to bother looking for her. He didn't want any ties to him. I had no references, no family. I went down to the pond behind the house, filled my pockets with stones and walked into the water."

"Hawthorn trees are sacred, but you already know that."

Nuala nodded.

"The berries are good for the heart; help with angina and arrhythmia. They're used to treat insomnia, anxiety, and indigestion. They are also high in antioxidants, vitamins and minerals —"

Nuala cut her off. "I know all that as well. But why do you think it might have meaning in a familial sense, like in my dream where it was used as a family tree?"

"That's understandable. It's a symbol of hearth and home. It represents courage and determination. In moon astrology, it's associated with the Mansion of the Hearth, which represents family togetherness, nurturing and home."

"Ah, I see. Now that makes sense."

"Are there any hawthorn trees on this property?" Deirdre asked.

"I'm not sure. That would be a good exercise — survey the property and look for hawthorn."

The sisters continued their walk, skirting the forest area and meandering down towards the pastureland. Nuala filled Deirdre in on the new acquisition of 'Mahogany,' as they watched the stallions grazing in the field. They sat for a moment to watch the majestic creatures as they grazed. Deirdre's eyes roamed the edges of the pasture where it met the treeline.

"Let's walk a while over that way …" she said as she stood from the fallen log they were sitting on.

"Did you see something?" Nuala asked.

"Possibly. I'm curious. See that stump about thigh high over there? It looks suspiciously like a hawthorn …"

They walked closer to the stump and Deirdre observed, "See these ridges and fissures in the bark? This was a very old tree. It was cut with an axe, not struck by lightning or fallen from decay."

"Isn't that bad luck? To cut down a hawthorn?" Nuala asked. "I remember a story recently about having to reroute a motorway because of a controversy over a hawthorn tree in the original path that would need to be cut down."

"Exactly. Cooler heads prevailed and the tree was spared. The motorway was rerouted several metres. If this was cut in McGuire's time, it would explain the bad luck and horrible things that happened here."

"You're kidding, right?" Nuala said with a nervous laugh.

"Only partially. I personally wouldn't mess with the fairies!" Deirdre said with a grin. "But it is in no way an excuse for bad behaviour on the part of wicked men."

The two women turned back towards the house. As they walked, they came upon another stump, and another … In all, five trees, all hawthorns according to Deirdre, had been cut not far from the treeline.

"It looks like these were cut to enlarge the pastureland. I wonder if Seán can find a record of it in the house account books," Nuala mused.

The sisters returned to the house to find Seán and Moira in the parlour. When they entered, Seán jumped up from his chair and came to greet them.

"I'm so glad you're back! I was about to go hunt you down," he said.

"Why? What's wrong?" Nuala's worried look caused Seán to quickly explain.

"Nothing is wrong, acushla! But Moira was waiting for you to come before she will share what she just experienced upstairs with your visitor. I am dying to know!"

"Ah! We are all ears, then!" Nuala said as she and Deirdre hurriedly crossed the room to sit next to Moira on the couch.

"Her name is Mairéad. That should be an easy one for you to find traces of in the archives, Nuala," Moira began. "She worked as a maid here under William McGuire, who took advantage of her."

"I knew it! Deirdre and I both guessed he might be the culprit!" Nuala said.

"He'd been trying for ages to have a son, but after two dead wives and multiple miscarriages, he began looking elsewhere for an heir. He got Mairéad pregnant about the same time he learned his third wife, Oona, was pregnant as well. Oona gave birth to John, and days later, Mairéad gave birth to a girl. He said he didn't need a daughter; he already had his heir. He took the child and kicked Mairéad out."

"What a monster!" Nuala exclaimed.

"Heartless," Deirdre agreed. "What did she do?"

"She drowned herself in the pond."

Stunned silence followed this announcement. Then Seán said, "The pond on the property? It's not so deep …"

"We may just find it was larger fifty years ago, but

no matter, she loaded up with rocks and made it work."

"But what about the child? Does Mairéad know what happened to her?"

"For the short time she had her, she named her Croía. 'She stole my heart,' Mairéad said. But she doesn't know what William did with her or, if she did survive, what name she was given. And that, my dears, is the sorrow that is keeping her from moving on."

"What did you tell her?" Nuala asked.

"I told her I would help her, of course. Now I need *your* help to accomplish that!"

Chapter 5

*Cuir síoda ar ghabhar agus tá sé fós ina
ghabhar.*
Put silk on a goat and it's still a goat.

—Irish Proverb

"Does everyone know their assignments? Shall I review?" Moira asked as she and Deirdre were about to drive back to Dublin.

"I'm checking civil registration for a death record for Máiréad in 1958," Nuala said. "Nineteen-fifty-nine is the last year that civil registration records are available online, so that's lucky."

"You might also look for an infant death during the same time period," Moira said.

"You don't think he murdered the child, do you? And if he did, he certainly wouldn't have the death recorded," Deirdre reasoned.

"You're probably right. I just don't put anything past what a McGuire male will do to anything or anyone who gets in his way," Moira said. "There might be a birth record for her though, if she was adopted."

"Without knowing what name the baby was given by her adoptive parents, any search for her birth will be near impossible. As far as we know, Croía is only the name Mairéad gave her, but not necessarily what would have been recorded in church baptismal records."

"I'm looking for adoption records for the same time period," Deirdre said. "But I'm not very hopeful, as I'm thinking McGuire would have done something privately, not through official channels."

"I'm not sure why, but I'm going through the McGuire account books for … what am I looking for?" Seán asked, looking sheepishly at Nuala.

"Payments out, of an unspecified or unusual nature, maybe on a regular basis that may indicate William was paying for Croía's upkeep. Also, any record of payment for taking down the hawthorns," Nuala said.

"How does that tie into the ghost?" Seán asked.

"It doesn't, directly. I just want to know who we have to blame for any negative karma here," Nuala said. "And I have a mind to plant a forest of hawthorns to make it up to the fairies."

Seán started to laugh, but as no one joined him, he quickly sobered. "Okay, I'm on it."

"Want to meet back here next weekend?" Nuala invited.

"Brunch again? We certainly don't mind being your testers for new recipes!" Deirdre said.

"It's a date, then," Nuala said. "See you next Sunday!"

In the Mini Cooper on the way back to Dublin, Deirdre pressed Moira for more insights into the apparition. "What was she like? How did she seem? What was her attitude towards William McGuire?"

"She was calm, resigned, but determined. She didn't seem to harbour resentment against McGuire. She stated things matter-of-factly, without emotion. She wants to know what happened to her daughter, what her life has been like. I believe she wants her daughter to know her, or, I should say, of her — that she was the one who gave her life. A simple, understandable desire."

Deirdre, tasked with exploring what happened to Croía, said, "Let's lay out the options. McGuire would have most likely placed the child quietly with someone loyal to him; someone whom he could trust. Alternately, he *could* have 'disposed' of the infant, but that seems extreme and unnecessary."

"Maybe he just abandoned her to the church — left her on the doorstep of the rectory, type thing," Moira suggested.

"If that's the case, local parish records may have an entry for a baptism of an anonymous infant." Deirdre was lost in thought, absentmindedly twirling a lock of hair around her finger that had come loose from her ponytail, then mused, "I wonder if William's wife, Oona, was aware of who fathered Mairéad's baby?"

"That's a good question. Mairéad didn't say, just that she was only allowed to remain at the house until her baby was born, then she had to leave."

"That poor woman! I can't get the image of her walking into the lake out of my mind."

"It's sad, but it's tempered by the understanding that she is still who she is — still a being with feelings and desires that we have an opportunity to help," Moira said.

They arrived home just as Billy, their dog-sitter, was returning with Suki from an outing at the park. He let Suki off leash to run to Deirdre, her person, for a welcome-home greeting.

"How's my best girl? I see you! You're amazing, yes you are!" Deirdre cooed at the Anatolian Shepherd who idolised her. "Everything go okay?" she questioned Billy.

"Just grand! She met up with her favourite playmates at the park and had a good romp for an hour or so before tiring out."

"Thanks so much for taking her out. We'll be gone same time next Sunday as well, if you're available," Moira said.

"Sure thing; see you then!"

When they'd gone inside, Deirdre got out the remains of the apple bread and cut a slice for herself.

"Want a piece?" she offered Moira.

"That would be grand, along with a cuppa, if you are in a serving mood."

They sat at the kitchen table and continued their strategy discussion.

"Where do you think we should start our search for Mairéad's baby?" Deirdre asked.

"I like the idea that William could have dropped her off at a church. Let's map out the congregations — McGuires were Catholic, so let's start there — and begin visiting each one," Moira replied. "You do think we should visit in person, right?"

"We could see if any of the area records are available on microfilm first. That would be faster."

"Let's check with Ma to see if she knows the answer to that," Moira suggested.

A quick call to their mother, Dymphna, got the answer they didn't want to hear — only church records up through the end of the 1800s have been microfilmed. Civil registrations, on the other hand, were filmed up through 1959. Dymphna and Nuala were checking those.

"It's in person for us, then. We'll have to have our story straight, to gain access," Deirdre said, upon ending the call.

"Do you have a proposal for a spiel?" Moira asked.

"Well, let's not say a ghost sent us to look for her stolen baby, alright?" Deirdre said, only half in jest. Moira tended to be painfully honest about her gift when dealing with those from whom they wished to gain information.

Moira smiled, accepting her sister's teasing good-naturedly.

"I was thinking of just going the family history route. People searching for their Irish roots is such a popular activity nowadays, if we just say we're doing a family history search we should be okay. It's not so ancient history though, that I hope we don't come up against the privacy argument. Someone born in 1958 could still be alive today. Maybe we don't give a specific date unless pressed," Moira said.

They pulled out a map of the Kildare area — they liked the tactile approach of seeing all the towns spread out before them — then stuck flagged pins labelling where the Catholic churches were located. They identified nine congregations that were within a five-mile radius of the McGuire estate.

"These are pretty spread out. I think we should call ahead and make appointments to not waste time," Deirdre said. As a person of action, she then did just that, obtaining appointments for the next day with four of the nine, leaving messages with the others.

With their plan in place, they then focused their attentions on the mundane tasks they left undone when they headed to Kildare that morning.

CHAPTER 6

———

Tagann an t-ádh i sruthanna caola, mí-
ádh i dtaoidí rollta.
Good luck comes in slender currents,
misfortune in rolling tides.

—Irish Proverb

Nuala had been on speaker with Dymphna for over an hour as they went through online websites, combing through records to piece together the McGuire family tree. They had done this before, when they had worked together to discover Patrick Mahoney's ancestry, the spirit who had first come to their attention at the McGuire estate. Back then, almost eighteen months ago, they had made a good team, with Dymphna coaching and Nuala getting her feet wet as a genealogist. Now Nuala was more confident and just needed her mother's guidance now and again.

"Well, that's that! I think the discovery of William's

older sister is the best bet for where he most likely placed Mairéad's child," Nuala said.

"His sister's daughter, you mean. Mhuireann McGuire Lynch would have been sixty-eight in 1958 — too old to have plausibly given birth to or raised an infant. But her daughter, Briena Lynch Dempsey, at thirty-eight would be the likeliest candidate," Dymphna said. "She was married to Eoin Dempsey in Newbridge in 1950. If they remained in the area, that's the next major town over from Kildare, just on the other side of the Curragh."

"This is great, Ma. I can't wait to call Deirdre and Moira to tell them what we found. Thanks so much for your help."

"You're very welcome, mo chroí. Anything I can do to assist a distressed spirit, I'm happy to contribute."

Nuala laughed, "Ma, you're a natural! You should be an official partner in Gallagher Investigations!"

"I do what I can but am happy to leave the rest to my girls. Tell your sisters to watch themselves, as they have learned not all spirits are of the friendly type."

"Heya, it's me," Nuala said once she got Deirdre on the phone. "I've got news that couldn't wait until Sunday."

"What's the story?" Deirdre replied. She and Moira were on the road, Moira driving, to their next appointment at St. Brigid's Catholic Church in Suncroft. They were working their way from the periphery in towards Kildare. Their first stop at the Church of the Sacred Heart and Saint Brigid in Kilcullen had yielded no results, even though they had been given free rein in the records room.

"We — Ma and I — have learned that William had an older sister, born in 1890. Her name was Mhuireann. She married Michael Lynch, and they had a daughter, Briena, born in 1920. With no other relatives in the area that we could see, it seemed logical that William might bring the child to his niece to raise. She would have been about thirty-eight at the time, a reasonable age to raise a child."

"Fair play! Any idea what this Briena's married name might be?" Deirdre asked.

"She married Eoin Dempsey in Newbridge in 1950."

"So … Briena Dempsey. I don't suppose it specified what church they married in?" Deirdre pressed.

"Sorry. Civil Registration isn't the same as the church records; those details aren't given."

"Ah. That's okay, this is a great start. We have a couple churches in Newbridge we are checking out today, maybe we'll get lucky. Anything else?"

"Not yet, but we are still digging into the family," Nuala replied.

"Keep up the good work!"

"Slán."

Deirdre turned to Moira and said, "We're almost at St. Brigid's in Suncroft. That's less than ten kilometres from Newbridge. It's possible they could have had the child baptised down here."

They pulled into the church car park. As they approached the rectory, Moira said, "You did such a great job with the 'spiel' at our last stop that I think you should continue being the lead."

"Sure, I will."

They rang the bell, and the door was soon opened by the parish priest himself.

"Deirdre?"

"That's me. We spoke on the phone. And this is my sister, Moira."

"Nice to meet you, I'm Father Dunne. So, you're researching your family tree, eh?"

Deirdre smiled but didn't reply. On the phone she had just said they were doing family history research. She didn't want to say it wasn't exactly her *own* family they were researching.

"I'm afraid the books are not very organised. Not

much time in the day for clerical jobs like that, you know? If you've got the time to sort through the lot, and you're not allergic to dust, I'll take you through to the storage room."

Father Dunne left them at the entrance to a small room with no windows and one electric lightbulb hanging from the ceiling. There were bankers' boxes lining the walls that at least had date labels on the outside. Two chairs were also barely visible due to the piles of books on the seats.

"This could take *hours*," Moira moaned. "Where do we start?"

Deirdre had already moved to the bankers' boxes and, with her head tilted to the side, was slowly moving along the row reading the date labels.

"We find the year 1958," she replied.

Five minutes later they had the designated box pulled out and were sorting through the registers. "Here!" Moira called out. "*Baptisms 1958.*"

Not knowing in which month Croía was born, she started in January. Deirdre pulled out the baptismal book for 1959. "Just in case they weren't in a particular hurry to get the child baptised," she reasoned.

It took them the better part of an hour, but when they had finished, with no likely entry, they decided to swap books, to be sure they hadn't missed it.

A half-hour later, Deirdre closed the register and

said, "If we don't leave soon, we'll be late for our next appointment." She slid the slim volume into its proper spot in the box.

"Okay," Moira sighed, placing her register in as well. "It's more likely they attended a church closer to Newbridge, anyway."

They stopped at the rectory and thanked Father Dunne, then headed to their next appointment at St. Brigid's of the Curragh, which was only ten minutes away.

They were met by the curate who greeted them and ushered them into an office, then invited them to sit. They sat and looked expectantly at him.

"I hope this isn't a futile visit for you. When the secretary took your call, she was supposed to ask what years you were interested in searching." He looked expectantly at them with raised eyebrows indicating this was a question.

"We'd like to see records of baptisms for the years 1958 and 1959," Deirdre said.

He sighed heavily. "First there was the fire in 1922 that destroyed everything. We were in a temporary building for years and those records, between 1922 and 1959 are spotty at best. Many people in the area chose to worship elsewhere."

"We would appreciate a look at the 1959 ledger anyway, if possible," Deirdre said.

"Alright then, I'll bring it to you. Please wait here," he

said and left them.

"Not holding out much hope here," Deirdre said.

"You never know," Moira replied.

But they did know, soon enough. There were only eighteen entries for the year 1959, beginning in April of that year, and none could even remotely be Croía.

Back on the road, they had high hopes for results in St. Conleth's parish church.

"Considering Nuala's news that William's niece married in Newbridge, St. Conleth's would be the most likely place. Do you think she's still living? She'd be in her nineties," Moira mused.

"We'd have to check more current obituaries to find that out — What was that?" Deirdre interrupted herself as the car gave a jolt and veered to the left. Moira pulled hard on the wheel to correct and slowed the car to a stop on the verge. The two got out and peered at the left front tyre that was quickly going flat.

"Oh, no! I must have run over some broken glass — look here, there's a slash in the tyre."

"We're not going to make that appointment now. I'll check the spare, but it's going to take a while to change this out. It's been donkey's years since Da taught me how to change a tyre and I've never had to practice it," Deirdre admitted.

The spare was soft, but it would hold. The nuts were tight, and it took some effort before Deirdre could get the flat tyre off. For the rest of the way they drove under fifty kilometres per hour as the spare was not standard size.

Once in the town of Newbridge, they found a tyre centre and limped in. Upon examination they were told the flat was not reparable. A replacement would need to be ordered and wouldn't arrive until the next day.

"I could sell you four new tyres of a different brand, but you've still got plenty of tread on these. I don't advise putting a different type on, but I can get a match from a dealership in Kildare overnight."

"Looks like we're bunking in Newbridge for the night, then," Moira said. "I really don't want to have to buy four new tyres."

"There's a bed and breakfast nearby I'm sure will put you up reasonable for the night," the mechanic said. "It's within walking distance."

He gave them directions and they headed out, leaving the Mini Cooper in his care. They walked about a half mile and came to a store where they were able to acquire the minimum for an overnighter: toothbrushes and toothpaste for both women, and chamomile tea for Deirdre to ensure a good night's sleep.

Deirdre had called St. Conleth's rectory to tell of their

plight and cancel their appointment. Now, ensconced in their room at Cassie's Bed and Breakfast, they called back to reschedule for the following day. Her next call was to Billy, asking him to take Suki to his house overnight. He readily agreed. He and Suki were best mates. Although it wasn't late, they decided not to explore the night life within walking distance, as the day's events had exhausted them both. They'd get a good night's sleep and start again in the morning.

Newbridge, with a population of 21,000 was no small village, but the centre of town consisting of the church and shopping area was compact and easily negotiated on foot. The next morning they found it was an easy fifteen minutes' walk from their bed and breakfast on College Park Road to the church. As they came to the bridge over the River Liffey, they could see St. Conleth's on the other side of the river. Moira stopped and looked down into the water.

"I'm thinking we are going to find something here. The opposition we've experienced is an indicator of good things to come," she said.

"It sure seems that way sometimes. It's like we appreciate the good times more when it takes going through a hardship first. I hope you're right," Deidre replied.

The opposition didn't end once they entered the

church. They were to meet the person in charge of the records inside the church itself, but when they entered, they found themselves alone. Standing just inside the doorway, they looked up at the vaulted Gothic ceiling with its pointed arches, leading the eye to the glorious stained-glass window overlooking the altar. The simple wooden pews in between were a stark contrast. As they gaped at the beauty surrounding them, they heard the door open behind them and turned to see a woman enter. She was most likely in her fifties, greying hair pulled back in a bun and a stack of books in her arms.

"Are you my eleven o'clock appointment? I'm Ms McCarthy. Father Kelly has asked me to take you to the office. He had another appointment earlier, which is why I asked that you come here first."

"This is a beautiful church, it must have a rich history," Deirdre said.

"We are fortunate to have so many artworks here glorifying God. I'm glad you appreciate it," Ms McCarthy said. "Come now, the records are in the rectory."

Moira and Deirdre followed her to the building next door and were ushered into an office. Ms McCarthy pulled out some forms from a drawer in the desk and placed them in front of the sisters.

"I just need to have you fill out these forms with

the name of the person who was baptised, the date of the baptism, and your relationship to them."

"We don't actually know the name and date; we were hoping to be able to browse the entries," Deirdre said.

"So, this is not for someone you know? I'm confused …"

"We are doing a family history search for a client," Deirdre explained.

"You are not related to the person you seek then?"

When neither responded, she continued. "I'm sorry, but for privacy reasons, we cannot give out that information. You'll have to return with the relative of the person who was baptised."

Moira was about to protest, or explain further who their "client" was, Deirdre wasn't sure which, but not trusting her to be anything but honest, she interrupted.

"Thank you for seeing us. We're sorry to have wasted your time."

With that, the sisters turned and left the room. Once back in the Mini, Moira said, "There seems to be a wide range of protocols at these individual churches. There's not one consistent policy for searching the records."

"This 'protocol' continues the opposition you mentioned earlier, for sure. Any ideas what to do next?"

"It might be time to call in reinforcements."

Chapter 7

Ní iasc é go dtí go bhfuil sé ar an mbruach.
It's not a fish until it's on the bank.

—Irish Proverb

"Or, maybe we don't need a baptismal record. Now that we know William had a sister, let's focus on finding out what happened to her," Moira suggested.

"Are you reluctant to ask Nana Brigid for help?" Deirdre asked, eyebrows raised.

"She's always told me we have the ability to figure things out for ourselves; that we need to exhaust all our options, then she will step in. I don't feel like we've reached that point yet, do you?"

"You're right, and with Nuala and Ma helping out, we need to give it a lash before running to Nana Brigid."

"When we get back to the room, let's first check with

the tyre shop to get an update on the Mini, then we can call Nuala and see if she's come up with anything new."

"That's sound," Deirdre agreed.

The Mini was just being calibrated and it would be ready in thirty minutes. While they waited, they spoke with Nuala. She had indeed discovered a few things. Michael Lynch, William's brother-in-law and husband to Mhuireann McGuire, had been a steward in the Turf Club back in the 1920s and 30s, enforcing the Rules of Horse Racing at the Curragh.

"Nice for her father, Hugh, to have a friendly face on the inside. Although he's the one who transitioned the estate to breeding instead of racing, correct?" Deirdre remarked.

"Hugh inherited the operation in 1905 at the death of his father, but I believe he transitioned to breeding in the 1920s. It seems logical that Mhuireann would have met her husband at the racetrack, at least. They would have been in the same circle of acquaintances. I've checked for children born to their daughter, Briena, and her husband, Eoin Dempsey, but come up empty. They were married in 1950, so by 1958 they may have been more than willing to take an infant if they hadn't any of their own."

"That's plausible. What kinds of records could we look at that might reveal they were raising a child … any child?" Deirdre asked. "That is, without looking at church records, as we've run into a dead end there unless we already know everything we are looking for."

"Let me talk to Ma and I'll get back to you."

"Right. Love you! Bye! Bye!"

"Byebyebye!"

Once they'd disconnected, Moira said, "I've been thinking … what about newspaper announcements? We could look for an engagement or marriage notice for a daughter of the Dempseys. Or sometimes back then in smaller communities like this, there were sections of local news like who was visiting whom and who graduated from uni, etc. Those we can access on microfilm, at least."

"Brilliant! Can you check the Newspaper Archives to see what's available for those years?"

"I don't have my computer with me, but I saw a station in the front room that is available to guests. Let's use that," Moira said.

Fifteen minutes later they ascertained that the microfilmed newspapers only went up to 1950.

"Out of luck again!" Deirdre sighed.

The proprietor, Cassie Bell, came in from the hall and asked if she could help with anything.

"Can you tell us what the local news publication is for this area?" Deirdre asked.

"There's the Newbridge Now Weekly," she offered.

"Their office is on Liffey Terrace, around the corner from the library."

"Spot on! That's what we need to hear!"

"Will you be staying another night, then?" Cassie asked.

"We'll be heading out in a few minutes. Our vehicle is repaired, so we'll pick that up then head over to the Newbridge Now office. That will hopefully conclude our business here and we won't need to stay another night. It's been lovely, though. Thanks so much for your help," Deirdre replied.

"Feels good to have the Mini back," Moira said as they pulled into the parking lot of Newbridge Now. "I feel like we're back on track."

"Let's hope we make some progress here," Deirdre added.

"You alright?" the clerk at the counter with the name badge of *Mary* said as they entered.

"We are wondering how far back Newbridge Now has been in operation," Deirdre began.

"The first issue came out in 1898," Mary said.

"That's grand! And have they all been digitized for viewing?"

"The oldest ones have been. They were too fragile

for handling, so they were filmed first to preserve them. Once the paper went online in 2000, they started working backwards from there. I think the project has gone back as far as the 1980s."

"You are saying that there's a gap between the oldest and the newest as far as digitisation?" Deirdre asked.

"That's correct. The years 1940-1979 are still only in hardcopy."

Moira and Deirdre looked at one another: *more opposition.*

"Is it possible to look at some of those hardcopy issues?" Deirdre asked, both sisters holding their breath for the answer.

"Of course. We have a reading room with the issues in binders. Are there specific dates you are interested in?"

With binders piled around them for the years 1958 through 1979, both women got to work sifting through all the local happenings in the Newbridge area.

"I'm so happy this is a weekly and not a daily!" Moira said.

Deidre laughed. "Always the optimist!"

They had only just started through 1958 when a headline jumped out at them: BODY OF UNIDENTIFIED DROWNING VICTIM FOUND ON THE BANKS OF THE LIFFEY.

Chapter 8

Caisleáin a thógáil san aer ...
Building castles in the air ...

—Irish Proverb

"This morning a woman's body was pulled from the Liffey, an apparent drowning victim. The woman had no identification on her, and only a ten-pound note in her pocket. She appears to be in her early twenties, long dark hair, blue eyes. Gardaí are requesting anyone with information that can help in their investigation to please come forward."

The byline was one Finn O'Farrell.

They set a page marker in the spot to get a photocopy and continued reading the next issue but no other information on the drowning appeared. In the following issue, two weeks after the body was discovered, there was a small notice that the still unidentified woman received a burial in St. Conleth's Cemetery. They marked that for photocopy as well.

Scanning the next several years for mention of anyone named Dempsey, nothing surfaced until 1973 where Moira came across the list of Newbridge students who had passed their state exams and received their Junior Certificate. One such student was named Bronagh Dempsey.

"Right age, right surname," Deirdre noted.

Three years later, Bronagh was listed as having passed the state exam for her Leaving Certificate.

"What we need is a wedding announcement that tells us who her parents are," Deirdre said. "Sometimes I say, 'wouldn't it be nice if …' and that helps to manifest what I want to have happen."

"I'm willing to try anything!" Moira said. "Wouldn't it be nice if we were to find a wedding announcement for our Bronagh Dempsey here."

Just then, Mary appeared behind them. "I was coming to see how you were getting on, and overheard you mention Bronagh Dempsey. There's only one Bronagh Dempsey in this town that I know of, and she's got her finger in just about every pie!"

"You know her? She's still alive? What can you tell us about her?" Moira asked.

"She's the Cathaoirleach of the town council; she's

on the board of directors at the library; she's the patron of the Riverbank Arts Centre. Just to mention a few. Why are you interested?"

Moira cautiously looked at Deirdre, who answered, "We are doing a family history search for a client who believes she might be related to Ms Dempsey. Does she live here in Newbridge?"

Mary seemed to regret divulging so much personal information to strangers and said, "Well, she has an office over at the town hall, I'm sure you could make an appointment to see her there." Then, looking at the bookmarked binders, she said, "Will you be wanting copies of these pages?"

The sisters nodded and Mary scooped up the items and left them.

"That was interesting. I wonder if Bronagh is well off, and Mary didn't want to aid and abet a needy relative coming out of the woodwork," Deirdre said.

"But she's alive! If she *is* Máiréad's child, what will we say to her when we talk to her?" Moira asked.

"I think we need to do more digging and be sure of our facts before we go there," Deirdre replied. "Let's ask Mary about Finn O'Farrell who reported on the drowned woman. If *he* is still around, he might have information we can use."

"Do we want to continue looking through the rest of these years while we're here?" Moira asked.

"That's a good idea. I got ahead of myself with this new development, but we should finish up here first."

"If she is going by Dempsey, that means she may not have married, but it doesn't hurt to look," Moira said. They each picked up a binder and returned to searching. Forty-five minutes later, halfway through 1979, Moira gave a little cry. "Ah! Here it is!"

She read: "BURKE – DEMPSEY WEDDING ATTENDED BY OVER 500."

She skimmed the article, pulling out the pertinent details, "James Tobey Burke, son of Clodagh and Torin Burke, owner of the champion racehorse, Torin's Pride, wed Bronagh Róisín Dempsey, daughter of Eoin and Briena Dempsey, in solemn ceremony at St. Conleth's on Saturday, June 10th, followed by a lavish reception at the Keadeen Hotel …"

"I wonder why she isn't Bronagh Burke now?" Deirdre mused.

"Divorce? Death? Kept her own maiden name?" Moira suggested. "What's important is that she is the daughter of Briena Lynch Dempsey, or should I say, 'adopted daughter'?"

"Bang on, Moira! Now let's find Finn O'Farrell."

At the front desk, they gave Mary the last binder to be copied. She returned with their copies and no mention of the subject of their search. When Deirdre asked her for a local phone directory, she retrieved that for them as well. Deirdre found one Finn O'Farrell listed and copied down the information. They thanked Mary for her assistance and left.

Outside the building, the sisters gave a 'Whoop!' and almost jogged to the Mini.

"Now that's what I call a productive research session!" Deirdre laughed. "Good thing you said that, *wouldn't it be nice*, bit!"

CHAPTER 9

———

*Ní chailleann tú an t-uisce go dtí go
bhfuil an tobar tirim.*
You never miss the water till the well has run dry.

—Irish Proverb

Nuala wasn't in the kitchen. She wasn't in the stables. She wasn't in the garden. Seán finally resorted to calling her mobile.

"Boutya?"

"Where are you?"

"I'm in the pasture planning out where to plant the new hawthorn trees."

"Ah. You don't waste any time, do you? I just barely ordered them yesterday."

"A good start is half the work, as Ma would say. If I have it all planned out, I won't waste time when they arrive. What did you call for? I'll be in soon to make lunch."

"I wanted to show you what I found in the McGuire accounts."

"I'll be right there!"

Nuala found her husband in his study, several old ledgers piled around him on the desk.

"Look here," he said, as soon as she entered. "First, the *Accounts Payable* for William McGuire beginning in 1935 when he inherited. There are regular payments to his sister, Mhuireann, marked 'inheritance payment.' He must have been instructed in his father's will to provide for her."

"That makes sense."

"But look, here in 1958, beginning in October, the payments doubled."

"Paying for the care of the child!" Nuala said.

"That's what I was thinking."

"And did you discover who cut down the hawthorns?" Nuala asked.

Seán pulled out another ledger from the pile that was much older, the pages yellowed and brittle. He opened to a page that had an orange sticky note on it. "Here in 1882 there's a notation for hiring workers to expand the paddock on the northwest side. That's the location of the main paddock where the stumps are located, right?"

"Fair play! That's it! So, 1882 — that would

have been Marcus McGuire. Like father, like son. That's generations of bad karma from the fairies."

Seán smiled, but then sobered. He took Nuala's hands in his and said, "C'mere to me. I've been thinking. When I was at the auction, I had to keep explaining who I was and from where. I'd say, 'you know, the old McGuire Stud Farm,' or 'Seán Kennedy from Kildare.' I want to newly brand our enterprise with something that is *not* McGuire, but sometimes I don't even feel myself a Kennedy, being not-quite-adopted by them. What do you think of *Hawthorn Place* or *Hawthorn House*? We could even call it *Hawthorn Estate* but that feels a bit too posh for me."

"G'way! You would do that? That should go a long way to making peace with the fairies, for sure!"

"So, what will it be? A place, a house?"

"You wouldn't want to call it *Hawthorn Stud*?" Nuala asked.

"I was thinking of that, but who knows how long we'll be in this business? I'd like to have a name that would carry on, regardless of what business is conducted here."

"Then I like *Hawthorn House*. 'Place' seems too generic. This house is our home. Seán, I'm totally gobsmacked! Thank you!" Nuala let go of his hands and threw her arms around his neck, kissing him soundly.

Chapter 10

***

Tugann am agus foighne seilide go Corcaigh.
Time and patience bring a snail to Cork.

—Irish Proverb

"Do you think we should call Finn first, or just show up on his doorstep?" Moira asked.

"Even if he were a budding young reporter in his twenties back in 1958, he'd be in his late seventies now. I don't want to give him a heart attack by just showing up. I'll give him a call," Deirdre said.

"You've reached Finn. Leave a message."

"Hello, my name is Deirdre Gallagher. My sister and I would like to stop by and visit you —" Before she could finish her message, the line was picked up.

"This is Finn, who is this?"

"Ah, so glad you are home. My sister, Moira, and I are in Newbridge investigating an old cold case you were reporting on back in 1958 —"

"The drowning. Not much else has happened here that you would call a 'cold case.' What can I do for you?"

"May we stop by to see you and discuss it?"

"I'm very willing to have a visit from two young ladies. Give me a few minutes to tidy up the gaff."

"We'll be along soon then. You're on the Ring of Roseberry?"

"Aye. I'm off the road a bit on the left; just outside the city limits."

"We'll find you!"

Twenty minutes later the sisters were driving down a long entrance to a comfortable looking home surrounded by sheep. An older man, possibly in his eighties, was standing by the front entrance.

"Howsitgoin?"

"Finn! I'm Deirdre Gallagher and this is my sister, Moira. Thanks for seeing us."

"Come in, come in," He indicated the door behind him and followed them into a cool, dark entry trimmed with mahogany wood. African masks lined one wall, and intricately woven baskets were stacked on the floor opposite.

Noticing their gaze, Finn said, "My souvenirs from the Congo. Right after the drowning death of that woman, I quit my job on the newspaper and joined the Defence

Forces. Then in 1960 we went to the Congo for the peacekeeping mission of the United Nations. I was at Jadotville during the siege and was a prisoner of war for a month. We weren't supposed to bring back stuff, but I figured I earned it."

He escorted them to a comfortable parlour with overstuffed chairs and stuffed deer and fox heads on the walls. Once they were seated, he indicated a tea service on a low table and began to pour.

With cup in hand, Moira asked, "Did you go back to the newspaper after your tour of duty was over?"

"Aye. But after fifteen years there they wanted to promote me to Editor-in-Chief at the retirement of the previous chief, but that's all deskwork and headaches. I loved being out in the field, chasing the story."

"Did you ever learn anything more about the woman pulled from the Liffey?" Deirdre asked.

"That was the strangest thing — not a word was ever said about it again. It's as if it never happened. No one came forward with information; there was no more police investigation; my editor didn't authorize any follow up." Here Finn leaned in closer to them. "I think there was a cover-up. *Someone* with influence wanted that story buried."

He folded his arms and sat back into his chair.

"Do you have any idea who would have that kind of influence?" Deirdre asked.

"The people with influence in this town are those associated with the Curragh. That's all I'm saying."

"Who do *you* think the woman was? Do you think there was foul play involved?" Moira asked.

"How can I *not* think there was foul play? You don't hush up something that is above-board. The fact that no one came forward to identify this woman could mean she wasn't local, meaning, not from Newbridge. We were a lot smaller town back then. Everyone knew most everyone. Why would someone not from here come here to drown herself? She had no wounds that would indicate murder, but back then our Anna Livia was awfully polluted. Even if I was about to end my life, I wouldn't do it in the Liffey. Just never made sense."

"Is there anything else you can tell us that would help us identify her?" Deirdre asked.

"Not that I can think of … oh, she's buried in yon cemetery at St. Conleth's; got a nice headstone paid for by the Dempsey family. They're both deceased now, but they were pretty big in the town — they referred to themselves as 'philanthropists,' giving back to the community and such."

Chapter II

—

Buail an t-iarann te.
Strike when the iron is hot.

—Irish Proverb

"That was interesting," Deirdre commented once they were in the Mini and headed back to town.

"Interesting is an interesting word choice. Dempsey paid for the headstone out of the kindness of his heart, or out of guilt for having received the stolen baby of the deceased?" Moira mused. "And how can we prove it?"

"Let's drive to the cemetery and see if we can locate her headstone," Deirdre suggested.

Arriving at the cemetery, they drove the aisles slowly, reading the larger stones until they came to the section corresponding with the timeframe of Mairéad's death. They parked in the roundabout separating sections and got out.

"You take that section, I'll start over here," Deirdre indicated. Less than half an hour later she called out, "Here! I think I've found it!"

Moira joined her in front of a tombstone that read, 'Here lies a young woman, taken from this life too soon. Rest in peace, your troubles are now over. Died November 1958 age approx. 22.'

"Sounds about right," Moira agreed. "It's too bad there wasn't an autopsy done. I'll bet they would have discovered she'd just given birth, and that the water in her lungs was *not* from the Liffey!"

"You would have made a great forensic pathologist, Moira. We've got no autopsy, so how are we going to connect the dots?"

"I think it's time we talked with Bronagh Dempsey."

"Ms Dempsey can see you at three o'clock next Wednesday."

"We're only in town for today, is there any way we can see her this afternoon?" Deirdre asked.

"I'm afraid not; she is in meetings for the rest of the day."

"Well, thanks anyway." After disconnecting, Deirdre said, "Implementing Plan B. We stake out the town hall offices and watch for Ms Cathaoirleach to leave, then follow her home."

"Seriously? I love it!"

It was already after two o'clock and they were both starving having missed lunch, so they stopped at a bakery and picked up something to eat in the car while they kept watch for Bronagh. Two hours passed, and Moira had begun to snooze when Deirdre poked her.

"That must be her. She matches the photo on the town council website. Look — she's getting into that black Range Rover."

Moira started the Mini and waited for the Range Rover to leave the parking lot, then followed at a distance. They drove south about six kilometres, then just past the Curragh, in the community of Ballysax, Bronagh turned into a gated drive, the gates parting as she turned. Moira sped up and followed the Range Rover through the gate before it closed behind her.

The Range Rover came to an immediate stop and Bronagh got out of the car. Standing with hands on hips, she looked towards the Mini. Both Moira and Deirdre got out of the Mini and walked to where Bronagh was standing.

"What do you think you are doing? This is private property!"

"We had to speak with you —"

"My office hours are ten to four, Monday through Thursday. Call for an appointment."

"We tried that but couldn't get an appointment until next week. We really need to talk with you about an injustice that has occurred and needs to be righted."

Bronagh looked at them pointedly, pausing a moment, then said, "An injustice, you say? Now I am intrigued. You might as well come in; you appear to be harmless, for stalkers!"

The three returned to their respective vehicles and Moira followed Bronagh down the long drive to the most impressive private home the sisters had ever seen. An Edwardian structure of at least 400 square metres, it stood centred on beautifully landscaped lawns. They were ushered into a foyer of white walls with white wood trim, set off by hand-knotted oriental rugs on timbered flooring.

Bronagh indicated a door to the right opposite the curved staircase and they entered an office space housing a desk, couch, fireplace and more timbered flooring accented with another oriental rug. The sisters sat next to each other on the edge of a white sofa, and Bronagh took an armchair opposite.

"Now, what is this all about?"

Moira looked to Deirdre, who nodded and said, "The body of a young woman was found on the banks of the Liffey not far from St. Conleth's Bridge. Although this appeared to be a suspicious death, nothing was done to investigate or bring anyone to justice for her death."

"When did this happen? I have not been informed of this! How did you hear about it?"

"It happened in 1958, and we learned the details this afternoon from Finn O'Farrell, the newspaperman who reported the story when it happened," Deirdre replied.

"Are you codding me? What has this ancient history got to do with me?"

"This 'ancient history' is *your* history."

Bronagh had been leaning forward in her seat, but now she sat back, her face appeared to have paled. Her voice came as a whisper, "You had better explain yourselves."

———

CHAPTER 12

Níor thachtadh an fhírinne fear riamh.
The truth never choked a man.

—Irish Proverb

Deirdre began, "You were born in 1958, correct? But are you aware that you were adopted by Eoin and Briena Dempsey?"

"How did you get that information? That is not something that is widely known outside of my family."

"But it's true, isn't it?" Deirdre pressed.

"I've always felt like I must have been adopted, but I wasn't told the truth until right before my mother passed. Some kind of deathbed conscience-clearing, I guess. But you haven't answered my question. How do you come by this information?"

"We have learned who your birth parents are and are tasked with the mission to let you know the truth of your birth."

"'The truth of my birth?' What does that mean?"

"Let me first ask you this: why did you feel that you were adopted?" Moira put in.

Bronagh sighed. "I guess nowadays they'd say I had 'abandonment issues.' Mother was distant emotionally, and Father was never around much. When they went on vacations together, I was always left with my nanny. I just didn't feel like they wanted me around. Then when Mother confessed that I was adopted, it all seemed to make sense. I must not have been wanted by my birth parents either."

"Did your mother tell you who your birth parents were?" Deirdre asked.

"She told me that my father was her uncle, my great-uncle William McGuire. She said she didn't know who my mother was — just that she was one of his paramours who died in childbirth and thus, William needed to find a home for me, as his wife wouldn't allow him to keep me."

"That is an interesting story, but only part of the truth. Thank you for confirming that William was your father, as we only had the word of your mother on that," Moira said.

"My mother? You have spoken with my birth mother? She is still alive?" Bronagh had once again moved forward to the edge of her chair.

"I have spoken with her, but, no, she is no longer living," Moira said.

"So, she died recently?"

"She died soon after you were born, but not in childbirth. After William took you away from her, in her desperation and destitution, she killed herself by walking into the pond on the McGuire property. Her body was later removed — by William, we assume — to the banks of the Liffey here in Newbridge, to erase any trace of her that would lead back to him."

"You are now referring once again to the drowning victim that was found here in 1958," Bronagh said. "It looks like we have come full-circle, and yet you still haven't told me how you were able to confirm this information from my birth mother when she obviously was dead before you were even born."

"Her spirit still resides in the house where she gave birth to you — the McGuire estate. She appeared to me, as I have the ability since childhood to see and converse with the deceased." Moira said this so matter-of-factly that for a moment, she thought Bronagh was just taking it all in, as she remained quiet.

Then Bronagh said, "Sorry? Would you repeat that please. I don't think I heard you correctly."

"We're not codding you, Bronagh. This is our

vocation. We formed Gallagher Investigations to help those who are deceased and have no other recourse to assist them with whatever is preventing them from moving on. My sister has a gift and has helped many souls as a result. We work closely with the Dublin gardaí in solving murders this way. Our liaison is Inspector Keating if you want further confirmation," Deirdre said.

"I believe your mother is not only stuck here on the earth but stuck at the McGuire house, as she doesn't know what happened to you and her grief is preventing her from moving on," Moira added.

"I am supposed to just believe you?" Bronagh asked.

"Your birth mother — her name was Mairéad Ashe — loved you and wanted you from the moment you were born. She named you 'Croía.' Mairéad said she never told William the name she gave you. You were ripped from her arms and whisked away to Newbridge from Kildare. Mairéad was a maid in the McGuire household. William had evidently given up on his wife, Oona's, ability to give him a male heir so he turned to Mairéad. Right before you were born, Oona did conceive and gave birth to a son, John. William no longer needed Mairéad or you, her child. He dismissed her from their service with only a ten-pound note and no references. Can you blame her for her actions?"

When Moira finished, Deirdre stood, and Moira, following her lead, stood to leave as well.

"Think about what we've told you," Deirdre said. "Call the Dublin gardaí and ask for Inspector Keating, she will vouch for us. We'd like to talk with you again, but we have at least delivered the information your mother wished you to know."

"Hopefully, Mairéad will contact me again, and I can let *her* know what has become of you," Moira added. She handed Bronagh her business card. "We will be heading back to Dublin now, but feel free to call us anytime, and if Mairéad does make contact again, would you want us to let you know?"

"Please," Bronagh said, in barely a whisper. She didn't rise to see them out, so Deirdre and Moira left her there to contemplate all they had said.

Chapter 13

Dhá thrian de chabhair ná misneach a thabhairt.
Two-thirds of help is to give courage.

—Irish Proverb

The sisters had barely passed through the gate at the end of the drive when Deirdre's mobile rang. "Hello?"

"Ms Gallagher? This is Bronagh. I would like to visit the McGuire house where you say I was born, and where you also say my mother's spirit haunts. Is that possible? I read about the death of the last McGuire, but I don't know who owns it or lives there now ..."

"It's very possible! Our sister, the other member of Gallagher Investigations, recently married the heir to the McGuire estate and they live there now. That's how we came into contact with your mother. Let us know when your schedule will allow a visit, and we'll work it out with Nuala and Seán."

"That would be grand. Thanks a million!"

"We'll be in touch. Slán."

Deirdre's next call was to Nuala.

"Heya! I was just about to call you! Seán has scoured the accounting books and has found increased payments from William to his sister about the same time of Croía's birth. Definitely an indication of paying for her upkept."

"That solidifies what we have found. Thank Seán for his efforts."

"What have you found?"

"We've found Croía. Her name now is Bronagh and after hearing what we had to say, she wants to visit the McGuire place where she was born."

"That's deadly! You mean she hadn't a problem with dealing with spirits? You did tell her of Moira's gift, right?"

"We did and she seems okay with it all. I think she is hoping to make contact with her mother."

"When will she come?"

"We're coordinating that with her now. Do you have any constraints on your time for a visit? We will, of course, come out with her."

"I'm sure we can work around what she needs. Just tell her when you give directions to look for a sign at the turnoff to the drive that says, 'Hawthorn House.'"

"What? How did you get Seán to go for that?"

"It was his idea! I was gobsmacked as well! But thrilled at the same time. I'm having a new sign made up immediately. But tell me about Croía — I mean Bronagh."

"As usual, even with some setbacks, the way opened for us to find her. Mairéad is buried in the local cemetery in Newbridge, and Bronagh is a mover and shaker in the town. She was a bit standoffish and wary at first, but I think she can feel what we told her was the truth. I think you'll like her. We'll talk later when I know what her schedule is for a visit."

"Okay. Love you, bye-bye, bye-bye."

Three days later, the caravan of Moira and Deirdre, followed by Bronagh, turned into the drive indicated by the sign, HAWTHORN HOUSE. As they pulled up to the entrance and disembarked, Nuala was on the doorstep to greet them.

"Welcome! I'm so glad you're here!"

"Nuala, this is Bronagh; Bronagh, our sister, Nuala Kennedy."

"Thank you for allowing me to visit," Bronagh said.

"Of course! Seán is in the pasture with the new stallion who has just arrived, but he may be able to break away a bit later to meet you. Come inside."

The group settled into the parlour and Nuala offered tea with an accompanying assortment of biscuits and cakes.

"Nuala, these look wonderful! Are we your testers again? I haven't seen this type of tea cake before," Deirdre said, holding up a slice of cake she'd chosen off the cart.

Nuala laughed. "Well, you caught me. I hope you'll be honest and let me know what you think. It's a sticky prune and date cake. It's more fruit than cake!"

Everyone tried the confection and were unanimously agreed it was a winner.

"Nuala, you have a real talent for this," Bronagh said.

"Well, thank you, but you didn't come here to be my taste-testers."

"I came to … I'm not sure why I came. It's just something I felt I had to do."

As they sipped tea and sampled pastries, Bronagh shared more of her life story. She had met her birth father only once, when she was about ten, not knowing her true relationship with him at that time. She had come into her father's study to find William there with her parents. William had gotten red in the face and yelled at her to leave the room; they were discussing things that weren't for her ears.

She'd left the room, but of course, that made her even more curious as to what they were discussing. She tried to listen in at the crack in the door but only heard fragments. It sounded like her parents were requesting money and William was not happy about it. He said something about 'the girl is not to inherit anything' of his. That had surprised her, because why should she inherit anything from him?

"The things I've learned from Moira and Deirdre have helped me to make sense of these things," she concluded.

"The estate records are also helpful in that way." Nuala brought out the ledger that showed the jump in payments which William made to his sister, Mhuireann, for her inheritance after September 1958, and laid it on the table before Bronagh.

"I was born September 29, 1958. Are you saying my grandmother received money that was supposed to be for me?"

"That's what it looks like. Are you aware of any help you or your parents received from your Lynch grandparents?" Nuala asked.

"I remember going with my Nana Mhuireann at the beginning of every school year and shopping for clothes and supplies. They bought me my first auto when I got my driving licence ... And all that time it was William McGuire's guilt money?"

No one answered, and as the question hung in the air, Moira put down her teacup and stood.

"Would you like to go upstairs and visit the room where your mother's spirit appeared?" she asked.

"I would."

The four women started up the stairs, with Nuala leading the way. At the top of the stairs, Nuala stepped aside and let Moira lead the way to the room with the bedstead and cradle. Moira put her hand on the doorknob, but the door flung open with a force of its own and Moira was hurtled backwards, crashing into the wall opposite.

CHAPTER 14

Is é an bealach is faide thart an bealach is
giorra abhaile.
The longest way round is the shortest way home.

—Irish Proverb

Bronagh screamed, while Nuala and Deirdre attempted to reach their sister. The space around them darkened and the two sisters had to grope along the wall until they got to Moira. As they knelt beside the dazed woman, all four of them heard the harsh whisper that seemed to grate on their ears but only Moira could understand the words.

Desist! You are meddling with what you don't understand. Your interference is tarnishing my legacy and my family's name —

Moira struggled to her feet. With her sisters holding onto her, she raised her arms up high, as she had done once before when confronted with the angry spirit of Philip McGuire. She seemed to gather strength, and cutting off the harsh sound that filled the hall, she commanded,

"In the name of the Divine One, I release you to the angels, never to return, never to be replaced. Angels of Light, I call upon you to escort this troubled spirit from this realm to a place of learning where he may develop goodwill towards all, the living and the dead."

Moira staggered back, but her sisters kept her from falling. The darkness dissipated and the voice of William McGuire was silenced. In its place, a soft whisper that only Moira could hear said, "Thank you. You have released me from that man's influence once and for all. I feel like I am no longer tied to this place."

Moira answered, "Mairéad, your daughter is here. She is called Bronagh Dempsey, and she now knows your story."

The spirit looked to where Bronagh was standing at the top of the stairs, holding on to the railing as if her life depending on it. Moira motioned for her to come to her and Bronagh let go and walked shakily to where the three sisters stood.

"Is she here?" she whispered.

"She is. She says she is now free to move on."

"Mother? Thank you for giving me life. I'm sorry

your life was so sad and so short, but you will be remembered and honoured."

"My beautiful girl! Slán go fóill, mo stór. I will see you again in the Otherworld one day."

"There was a change in the air, and Bronagh asked, "Is she gone?"

"She is." Moira repeated to Bronagh her mother's last words.

Bronagh let out a cry and sobbed, "I just found her and lost her again."

"But you know her now, that she loved you and loves you still. Love doesn't end at death," Moira affirmed.

Two months later, Moira and Deirdre received an invitation in the mail to attend, as the special guests of the Newbridge cathaoirleach, the unveiling of a new monument for the previously unknown drowning victim of 1958.

Many dignitaries turned out, as well as the citizens of Newbridge and surrounding area. As much as Bronagh had tried to keep her actions under wraps until the unveiling, her request to have the body exhumed and tested for a DNA match to herself was sufficiently leaked that the big news was not really news at all.

As Bronagh stood in front of the grave, the hush belied the size of the crowd surrounding her. Speaking into a portable microphone she said,

"For too long, the occupant of this grave has been unnamed, unknown, forgotten. She was found on the banks of the Liffey, the victim of an apparent drowning. Nothing else was known about her and nothing else was done to discover more. I am here to rectify that. DNA testing has been done on her remains. The results conclusively indicate that the woman buried in this grave is my mother. No, not Briena Dempsey, whom you all knew, but my birth mother. Her name was Mairéad Ashe. She was alone, abandoned by the man who fathered me and took me from her. Today we might say she had post-partum depression, although being destitute and alone would be enough on its own to bring one to despair.

"Thanks to Nuala Kennedy, who was able to obtain the information of Mairéad's birth, and her sisters, Moira and Deirdre Gallagher, of Gallagher Investigations, who learned of the circumstances of Mairéad's death, we can now confidently reveal her to you."

At that, Bronagh pulled off the cloth covering the gravestone to display a highly polished marble marker which read:

HERE LIES THE EARTHLY REMAINS OF MAIRÉAD ASHE, BORN APRIL 28, 1936. DIED NOVEMBER 3, 1958. BELOVED AND HONOURED MOTHER, REST IN PEACE UNTIL WE MEET AGAIN.

A DEATH DOWN UNDER

Chapter 15

Tarraingíonn scéal scéal eile.
One story leads on to another.

—Irish Proverb

September 2012

"Bronagh! Good to hear from you! How are things in Newbridge?" Deirdre was out for a jog in Phoenix Park, but took the call when she saw the ID.

"Did I catch you at a bad time? You sound somewhat breathless."

"I'm jogging, but I can multitask."

"I was hoping to schedule a consult with Gallagher Investigations."

"Certainly. What's happening?"

"It's not for me, but for a friend. I told her some of what you did for me last spring and she's hoping you can help her as well."

"Sounds intriguing. Can you come to Dublin? I believe we could fit you in tomorrow afternoon, if that works."

Deirdre had to smile to herself as she remembered how difficult it had been to try to get an immediate appointment with Bronagh when they were investigating her past. She was briefly tempted to push the date out, but this sounded too important to be petty.

"That would be grand," Bronagh said.

"I don't have my calendar on me, but when I get back home, I'll talk with Moira and confirm."

"I really appreciate that. Talk soon, byebye."

When Deirdre returned to the flat, she found Moira deep in invoices and bills pay folders, sorting out their finances. She looked up when Deirdre entered and asked, "How was your run?"

"Productive. I think I've got us a new client!"

"That so? That would be helpful," she replied, eyeing the papers strewn across her desk. "Anyone I would know?"

"Actually, an old client with a new request. Bronagh wants to bring a friend over for a consult."

"Really? Do you know what it's about?"

"Haven't a baldy notion. I pencilled her in for tomorrow. Does that work?"

Moira pulled up the calendar for Gallagher

Investigations. "Looks grand. Tell her half-one?"

Deirdre texted Bronagh with the update and got a thumbs up in reply.

The next day Bronagh arrived at the appointed time. Moira ushered her and her companion into the living room.

"This is my friend, Síofra. We work together on the city council," Bronagh began introductions. "Síofra, these are the sisters, Moira and Deirdre, I was telling you about."

"Nice to meet you; have a seat," Deirdre said, indicating the couch. "How can we help?"

"Thank you for seeing us. You're going to think I'm talking bollox, but Bronagh assures me you have the expertise I need."

Síofra paused, but when the sisters just continued to look at her encouragingly, she continued. "I think my sister has been kidnapped."

"That sounds like something you should take to the gardaí. What makes you suspect a kidnapping?" Deirdre asked.

"Nothing that would be taken seriously by gardaí. Riley is my baby sister. She finished uni last year and after working a while, decided to take some time to 'find herself.'

She flew to New Zealand to hike the Milford Track about a month ago. At first, she would check in with me each evening — our mother passed away when Riley was quite young, and I practically raised her. Over a week went by with no word, and I just assumed she was hiking in a remote spot that had no reception. But then last week I got a text from her saying she was low on funds and could I wire her a couple thousand euros."

"Was that out of character or something to make you suspicious?" Moira asked.

"Not only was it out of character — she prided herself on having saved the money she needed for the trip on her own and had carefully budgeted the total amount she planned for — but she used our secret names in the text."

"Secret names?" Deirdre prompted.

"Da's gone now too, but when we were young, he gave us names we were to use only when we were in trouble or had some kind of emergency. There are only the two of us, Ma having had several miscarriages between our births, thus the wide age gap. Da gave us names of the goddesses: I, being the oldest, am Danu, the mother goddess; Riley, who was quite the hallion when she was younger, is Clíodhna, the Queen of the Banshees."

"What did the text say, exactly?" Deirdre asked.

Síofra pulled up the text on her mobile and read:

"Danu, I'm in Christchurch and running low of funds. Can you spot me 2000 euros? Wire to the Western Union, City Centre. Love you, Clíodhna."

"Did you send the money?" Moira asked.

"I did. But since then, I have heard nothing more. Calls to her mobile go to voicemail. She would have sent something acknowledging receipt of the funds. Sweet Jaysus, Mary and Joseph! I told her not to make the trip alone, to take a friend. I even offered to go with her, but she can be so stubborn at times. She was determined to use the time for reflection and self-discovery; she said she couldn't do that if she had a companion along."

"Did you check with the Western Union office to learn if the funds were picked up and by whom?" Deirdre asked.

"I called and all they could tell me was that the money was collected."

Moira was lost in thought for a moment, then said, with deliberation, "Have you had any feelings that she is in trouble? Any dreams, premonitions, signs other than the secret names?"

Síofra looked at her with mouth agape before saying, "I saw her in a dream three nights ago. She was in a field, dressed in white. She beckoned to me to come closer, as she was trying to tell me something, but I couldn't hear her. When I got closer, I heard her say, 'bring me home.'"

Chapter 16

Ní féidir an dubh a chur ina gheal, ach seal.
You can only deny the truth, for a while.

—Irish Proverb

"It was just a dream, though. It doesn't mean anything, right? Why would you ask about such a thing?" Síofra asked.

"Nothing is ever 'just a dream,' especially in a situation like this," Moira said. "I don't have the resources to trace your sister's whereabouts. I think we need to call in the gardaí."

"But who is going to act on such slim evidence?"

"There is someone — a guard here in Dublin — who needs to hear your story," Deirdre said. "Let me call and see if Inspector Keating is available." She left the room to make the call and returned a few minutes later.

"She will see us. Shall we go now?"

The four women drove in two cars to the Dublin gardaí station and were escorted to an interview room where Inspector Keating soon joined them.

"Good to see you again, Moira, Deirdre. Who are your friends?"

Bronagh offered her hand. "Bronagh Dempsey, and this is my friend, Síofra O'Cleary. We are in the Newbridge town council. Thank you for seeing us."

"Are you here on council business?"

"Not at all. Gallagher Investigations helped me with a family matter a few months ago, so when Síofra made known to me her concerns, I immediately thought of them. But it seems they feel you could be of assistance as well."

"What's the story, Síofra?"

As Síofra recounted her tale, Inspector Keating listened intently without interruption until she recounted her dream. Then the inspector said, "Nuala should be here. Isn't she the dreaming expert in this company?"

"I think it's clear, don't you? Riley has met up with one or more gombeens. Could you request a look at her bank account to see about withdrawals and where they took place? That might help us know where she was last," Deirdre said.

"We can do that. I think it also warrants a check if

there are any surveillance cameras at that Western Union office in Christchurch."

"You would do that? On such little evidence?" Síofra asked.

"If the Gallaghers feel there is a suspicion of foul play, that's all I need. Leave your contact information with me and we'll be in touch when I have something to share."

With that, they were dismissed.

Standing next to their vehicles in the car park, Síofra asked, "How is it that you have such a great relationship with the gardaí?"

"Not 'the gardaí'— one guard. We have been working with Inspector Keating for some time now. We've helped her with several cases, so she returns the favour by helping us," Deirdre said.

"I'm impressed. But I get the feeling you think something bad has happened to Riley," Síofra said.

"I don't want to give you false hope. The fact that you are reaching out suggests you believe there's something terribly amiss as well," Moira said. "Let's see what Inspector Keating's investigation turns up and we'll go from there. Go home and let us know if you hear anything more from Riley."

"Spare no expense. Whatever it takes to find Riley, I will cover the cost as well as your fees," Bronagh said.

Síofra gasped. "I can't let you do that!"

"Of course you can. With the investigation taking place in New Zealand, the expenses could mount up quickly. I have the means, and it is on my suggestion that we have come to Moira and Deirdre. Think no more about it."

With that, the foursome parted. On the way home Deirdre asked, "What's your gut feeling on this?"

"The dream suggests she is already on the Otherside. I think I need to ask Nana Brigid about this," Moira said.

Moira dropped Deirdre off at the flat and drove to Donnybrook Cemetery, her favourite place to sit amidst the departed and seek assistance. This intimately small, shaded green spot, sheltered from the bustle of the city around it, provided a sense of peace and calm where she could quiet her thoughts and focus them on the Otherworld. She found a stone bench and settled in to wait.

She breathed in deeply, held her breath a moment, then let it out slowly. Concentrating on projecting her thoughts and intentions towards her Nana Brigid, her mentor and guide to the Otherside, she painted her grandmother's image in her mind.

"Conas atá tú, Moira?" The image that appeared

before her was much more glorious than she could envision, but it was her Nana Brigid. With no living soul around, Moira was free to speak openly to her grandmother.

"Fair to middling, Maimeó, but our new friend is not so well," Moira replied. Oh, how she wished she could embrace this beloved woman! She had never tried, sensing an unseen but impenetrable barrier between them.

"A new challenge has presented itself?"

"A young cailín has gone missing in New Zealand. Her sister is distraught and fears the worst. I must confess I believe that she has come to some harm. Do you know of a newly arrived spirit named Riley O'Cleary?"

"Do you know how many spirits transition to the Otherside at any given moment, my dear? The name is not familiar to me, but I can investigate and let you know. If it was a violent passage, she may be needing some assistance, which I can offer."

"That would be grand, Maimeó! I will follow the trail of the earthly route she recently took and await your return."

CHAPTER 17

An té nach gcuirfidh san earrach,
ní bhainfidh sé san fhómhar.
He who does not sow in spring, will
not reap in the autumn.

—Irish Proverb

When Moira returned to the flat, Deirdre was on a call with Síofra. Deirdre switched the mobile to speaker mode so Moira could hear as well.

"Inspector Keating just called. She asked for a picture of Riley to compare to the camera footage from Western Union when it arrives. I'll be back in Dublin tomorrow to bring the photos to her. I was hoping you would be there as well," Síofra said.

"What time will you be here?" Deirdre asked.

"She requested that I come at half-two."

Deirdre looked to Moira, who nodded. "That works for us. See you then. Look after yourself."

"Slán."

Once disconnected, Deirdre asked, "Did you have a nice visit at the cemetery?"

"Aye, it was grand! Maimeó came, of course, but she didn't know of Riley. She said she would look into it."

"Well, that's good news, right? It means she probably isn't dead yet?"

"Not necessarily. Nana B reminded me of how vast the Otherside is, and she doesn't know personally every spirit that enters."

"That makes sense. So now we wait."

"We wait, but we don't do nothing. Síofra said Riley was a part of a guided tour to hike the Milford Track. I was thinking we could call them and ask if she ever signed in, and if so, what days she was with them. That might narrow the search somewhat," Moira said.

"Good thinking. Do you remember the name of the outfit?"

"Extreme Hikes. I'll look them up."

While Moira engaged with the Extreme Hikes representative, Deirdre began searching online New Zealand newspapers for any references to recent crimes of violence. After about twenty minutes she called out to Moira, whom she noticed had just ended her call.

"Here's an article in *The Press* about bikie gangs in

the Christchurch area responsible for a string of robberies and assaults. They are warning people to be cautious when they withdraw money from ATM machines, especially in less populated areas. Several people have been robbed after receiving their money. I wonder if something like that could have happened to Riley."

"It would be nice to know if Inspector Keating has discovered anything about her bank account. Maybe we'll find out more when we go in with Síofra tomorrow," Moira replied.

"What did you learn from the outfitters?" Deirdre asked.

"The man I spoke to at first couldn't tell me much, only that Riley signed in on the tour that hiked the week before last. When I told him Riley was missing and feared in danger, he transferred me to a woman who had been on that tour as one of the guides. She told me she remembered Riley well, as there was an incident on the hike that caused quite a stir. It seems there was an individual in the group that continued to pester Riley with 'unwanted advances.' That's what she called them. He was always inviting her to hike with him or to take a detour with him or sit with him at meals. Riley didn't seem interested — he was somewhat older than her, and a bit rough — and she got progressively annoyed. After a few days when he wasn't taking the hint, she just blew up and told him to get lost and leave her alone."

"That's very interesting. Did she tell you the name of this persistent admirer?"

"She said she couldn't divulge that for privacy reasons. As far as she could see, the pox spent the rest of the hike sulking and avoiding her. Riley teamed up with another female who was also hiking solo, and they mingled more with the main group together."

"Perhaps Inspector Keating can get this guide to be more forthcoming. We'll pass this on to her tomorrow as well."

The following day right at half-two Moira, Deirdre and Síofra sat together in an interview room waiting for the inspector to arrive. Síofra showed them the photo she'd brought of Riley.

"This was taken last year at her graduation. She's so full of life! Look at that smile, with the whole world ahead of her. Jaysus! I pray she is alright!"

Inspector Keating arrived and apologised for keeping them waiting. "I was hoping this would arrive before I saw you and it just came in."

She laid out photos on the desk taken at the Western Union office, and Síofra placed her photo of Riley next to them.

"I don't understand," Síofra said. "That's not Riley, that's a man."

"Do you recognise him?" Inspector Keating asked.

"I don't know him. Is that who picked up my money?"

"He's got that hat pulled down and his head is tilted, like he is intentionally hiding his face," Deirdre observed.

"The person I spoke to at the Western Union office said the man came in with a signed note from Riley authorizing him to pick up the money. He also had her ID with him."

"Did they send you a copy of the note?" Síofra asked.

"It's here." Inspector Keating put another paper on the desk.

"That's Riley's signature and her driver's licence," Síofra confirmed.

Moira reported on her conversation with personnel at Extreme Hikes. "Perhaps you could get them to provide the name of the persistent fellow hiker?" she asked the inspector.

"I'm sure we can," Inspector Keating replied. To Síofra she said, "We received her bank information as well this morning. She has recently withdrawn a sizeable amount from her savings, leaving a balance of less than one hundred euros."

"What? She had close to ten thousand saved! She'd

budgeted about four thousand for this trip, then planned to invest the rest. Something is terribly wrong!"

"Was she still in Christchurch when she withdrew the money?" Deirdre asked.

"She was. I'll be coordinating with the New Zealand police, turning over this information to them. They will be better equipped to handle things on their end. Thank you for bringing in this information." Inspector Keating stood, dismissing the three women.

As they stood to leave, the inspector requested that Moira remain a moment.

"Have you heard anything from Riley?" she asked.

"Not yet."

"That's a good thing, right?"

"Not necessarily. Nana Brigid is searching for her on the Otherside just to confirm she hasn't arrived there. I hope to hear from her soon — Nana Brigid, that is, not Riley!"

As soon as Moira joined Deirdre and Síofra outside the station, Síofra asked, "So what's our next move?"

"You heard Inspector Keating, it's up to the New Zealand police at this point," Deirdre said.

"I can't just sit back and wait — we've got to do something. I'm going to Christchurch, who's going with me?"

CHAPTER 18

*Éist le fuaim na habhann agus
gheobhaidh tú breac.*
Listen to the sound of the river
and you will get a trout.

—Irish Proverb

True to her promise to finance the operation, two days later Bronagh delivered three tickets to Christchurch from Dublin, Business Class.

"I've never flown anything but economy before!" Síofra exclaimed.

"We haven't either but given the twenty-eight-hour flight time, I'm certainly grateful," Deirdre said.

They boarded at two o'clock on Tuesday afternoon and settled in for the long haul. Deirdre and Síofra shared a row, and Moira had an empty seat next to her. After several hours in the air, Moira took a turn in the jacks. When she returned to her seat, there was a woman sitting in the seat next to hers. But this wasn't just any woman …

Nana Brigid! Moira was proud of herself for not voicing her excitement aloud, but reverting instead to the mental spirit communication her grandmother had helped her hone. *I'm so happy to see you!*

And I, you, dear. I can't stay long, but wanted to let you know that your expedition is now one of retrieval and not rescue.

Ah. You have met Riley …

She arrived a few days ago but has been in an orientation specifically for those who were involuntarily helped into the Otherside. She doesn't have any desire for retaliation or revenge on her attacker; in fact, she seems quite serene and happy to be where she is. She said she tried to reach her sister but couldn't get through. I asked her if she wanted to visit with you, but she said just to give you the message that she would like to be brought home and buried in the family plot.

Does she not have any advice as to how we can find her, or at least who it was that did this? I'm sure the police would want that person off the streets to do no harm to others.

I agree with you that a visit would be helpful, especially seeing as you have embarked on this lengthy trip on her behalf. I will speak with her again and see if she will entertain a visit to provide some direction for you.

At that moment, the plane experienced some turbulence and Moira stiffened, grasping the armrests and holding her breath. At the same moment, her grandmother dematerialized without so much as a fare-thee-well.

Once the plane stabilized and the seatbelt sign had once again been turned off, Moira stood and leaned into the seating where her sister and Síofra were.

"I've had a visitor," she said softly.

"A visitor?" Síofra questioned, while Deirdre just raised an eyebrow.

"Maimeó said Riley is with her and she is hoping to get her to guide us to … where she is located so we can bring her home."

"Someone's found my sister? Where is she? Is she okay? Someone on this plane has seen her?" Síofra was out of her seatbelt and looking frantically around the plane.

A stewardess came by and asked Moira to return to her seat, and for Síofra to buckle up, as the seatbelt sign had once again been turned on. Moira left Deirdre to decide how much and what to tell Síofra about her contacts on the Otherside. Only a few minutes had passed before Moira could hear Síofra choke back a sob. She covered her face with her hands, but her shoulders shook, reflecting the emotional blow that she had just received.

After two layovers, one in Dubai and one in Sydney, they arrived in Christchurch on Thursday at eight in the morning. With plenty of time for in-depth discussion and education into the world of spirits, Síofra seemed to have calmed to the point of joy at her new-found understanding of her sister's whereabouts and condition.

While Deirdre retrieved their rental car, Síofra asked Moira, "She's truly happy now? She isn't angry at what has happened to her?"

"It's a common occurrence; the Otherside is a pleasant place for most people. Only the truly evil find themselves in a place of discomfort. And she is being well cared for; she's learning a lot."

"And you say she may visit you? Give you information that will help us find her … her body?"

"I'm hoping. We don't have a lot to go on, otherwise," Moira replied.

As soon as the three were settled in the car with Deirdre behind the wheel, they first drove to the Christchurch police station. Inspector Keating had given them the name of the person she had been in touch with — the officer in charge of the investigation into Riley's disappearance.

"We're here to see Officer Lee, please," Síofra said to the young man at the front desk.

"What is this about? Who shall I say is asking?" His name badge read, Wilson.

"I'm Síofra O'Cleary, from Ireland. Officer Lee is looking into the disappearance of my sister, Riley O'Cleary."

"Right, okay, I'll let him know."

Wilson disappeared behind a door to their right and was gone about five minutes. When the door opened and Wilson reappeared, he was followed by an older man with thick, greying hair around his temples and dark-framed glasses. He approached the women with an outstretched hand.

"Kia Ora! Sergeant Thomas Lee, at your service. Which of you is Ms O'Cleary?"

Síofra took his hand and shook it, then turned and said, "These are my friends, Moira and Deirdre Gallagher."

"Ah! Glad to meet you! Inspector Keating mentioned I should be on the lookout for the three of you. I hope you're not too exhausted from the travel."

"We're grand; what do you know about my sister's disappearance?" Síofra said, getting right to the point.

"Come back into my office where we can chat in private," he said.

They followed him down a corridor and entered a

room containing a desk and two chairs in front of it. Several other chairs lined the side wall. Sergeant Lee grabbed a chair from the side and moved it in line with the other two in front of the desk, then indicated they should sit, as he moved behind the desk. There were no windows in the room and Moira began to feel claustrophobic in the small enclosure. Deirdre glanced at her, then reached into her bag and handed her sister a mint — something to distract her. Moira smiled gratefully and popped it discreetly into her mouth.

"About my sister?" Síofra pressed, sitting on the edge of her chair, hands gripping the arm rail, as though ready to vault out and make a beeline to wherever Sergeant Lee indicated the next clue would be found.

"We followed up on the hiker who was harassing her. We got his name and address and he's been interviewed. He has a solid alibi for the week in question. He continued his vacation by hiking the Grand Tramp, which is a seven-day guided tour. He was nowhere near Christchurch when Ms O'Cleary picked up the wire transfer."

"Could he have had accomplices? Someone here to do his dirty work?" Síofra questioned.

"You believe someone attacked and, or robbed your sister to avenge Mr. Hobson's hurt feelings?"

"I don't know! I don't know! You're the investigator,

you should be checking all these things!" Síofra began wringing her hands. "I just want to find her!"

"Straight up, we all want to find her, and we are doing our best to that end," he said.

"What about the man in the Western Union office that collected her money?" Deirdre asked.

"We couldn't make a positive ID. He was intentionally avoiding the camera, which makes him even more suspicious. We have a description as best we could obtain from his clothing, height, and build and will continue to follow up there. Ms O'Cleary, I'm sorry you came all this way when there is nothing you can do here. We will let you know as soon as we find anything."

"And these bikie gangs that are in your city? Have they been detained and questioned? I understand there were several incidents of robberies that pointed to them," Moira asked.

"I see you have studied up on our crime issues, Ms Gallagher. We keep a close eye on the gang members, and yes, they have been questioned. The Western Union piece is not part of their MO, so that angle is not a likely one."

"Thank you for seeing us, Sergeant. We'll be staying at the City Centre Hotel for a few days. I hope you will keep us informed of any developments," Deirdre said as she rose from her chair. Moira rose as well, but Síofra just stared at them. Deirdre put out her hand to her and she took it, standing and moving with them to the door.

Once outside, Síofra turned to Deirdre, "I had more questions!"

"He obviously didn't have any more answers, or he would have said so. Let's regroup at the hotel and see where things stand," Deirdre said.

"You're right. And I *am* exhausted. Lead on," Síofra said, a note of resignation in her voice.

"We aren't giving up, Síofra. We'll find your sister. I'm exhausted as well, and hungry! I hope there's room service in the hotel — I don't feel up to a public restaurant right now," Moira said.

Upon check in they were informed that there was breakfast service, but no restaurant in the hotel for other meals, therefore no room service. The clerk identified several takeaway restaurants within walking distance, and while Moira and Síofra continued up to their room with the luggage, Deirdre went next door and picked up a pizza and salads from Mario's Authentic New York Pizza Parlour.

While they ate, they discussed what they might do to further the investigation. It was just past noon, and Síofra collapsed on the twin bed, vowing to only nap for a few minutes and to wake her in thirty if she wasn't up on her own. Deirdre said she had an idea she wanted to follow up on but wouldn't elaborate. Moira announced she wanted to walk through the Botanical Gardens they'd spotted on the way to the hotel, a mere kilometre away.

"How do you have the energy or inclination for sightseeing, Moira?" Síofra asked.

"It's more about finding a peaceful spot for introspection and contemplation than sightseeing," Moira replied. She wasn't ready to go into detail with Síofra on her methods for preparing to communicate with those on the Otherside.

"I'm going to the lobby to make a few calls, so I won't disturb your sleep," Deirdre said to Síofra. She and Moira went down the elevator together.

"What's your plan? Who are you calling?" Moira asked her sister.

"Did you happen to notice that the sergeant — unintentionally, I'm sure — dropped the name of the hiker?"

"Hobson! I did! What are you thinking?"

"I'm thinking of calling the Extreme Hiking Tours again and trying to get a bit more info from them," Deirdre replied.

"You aren't convinced of his innocence?"

"Not one hundred percent, yet …"

Chapter 19

An té a bhíonn siúlach, bíonn sé scéalach.
Travellers have tales to tell.

—Irish Proverb

"Hello, this is Nancy Hobson. My husband was on your hikes earlier this month and thinks he lost his silver cigarette case while there — possibly in the restroom of your centre in Queenstown? Has anything been turned in?" Deirdre asked the girlish voice that answered her call.

"I can check that for you, can you please hold?"

"Certainly! Thanks so much!"

The wait was short, and when the girl returned, she said, "There's nothing like that in lost and found, I'm afraid. Sorry."

"Oh, dear! It has great sentimental value. His father gave it to him just before he passed, God rest him! If it turns up, can you mail it to us? You have his address on file, right?"

"Hobson, you said?"

"He went on the Milford Track, then the Grand Tramp right after."

"Oh, right! Here it is: Daniel Hobson in Hornby, is that correct?"

"That's the one. I really appreciate your help, and thanks for looking," Deirdre said, as she ended the call.

There was no internet in the hotel, but the desk clerk gave her a map with the Tūranga Public Library circled — a five-minute walk from the hotel — where, he assured her, she would find public internet computers. Before heading there, she went back up to their third-floor room to leave a note for Moira, and Síofra, who was still asleep.

She found the library with no difficulty and logged onto the internet. Doing an address search for Daniel Hobson in Hornby, New Zealand, yielded only one name and address. Checking the map, she discovered that Hornby is a suburb of Christchurch, a twenty-minute drive from their hotel.

And Sergeant Lee didn't find that at all suspicious, even with a "solid" alibi?

Writing down the address and phone number, she made her way back to the hotel.

Moira enjoyed the twenty-minute walk to the botanical gardens after being cooped up in planes, airports, and offices for the better part of two days. The weather was cooperative, and she found the park surrounding the gardens without difficulty. As tempting as it was to go inside the greenhouse and stroll among the exotic plants, she chose instead to walk along the small lake opposite. She soon found an unoccupied picnic table in the shade of an ash tree. Cyclists, strollers, and joggers passed by as she sat and … waited.

I've been watching for you, my dear. I've brought someone I'd like you to meet.

A young woman materialised next to Nana Brigid. Moira recognised her from the photos that Síofra had brought to the garda station.

Riley! I'm so glad to meet you — well, sorry we have to meet this way, but I'm glad you've linked up with Nana Brigid. I'm sure she's taking good care of you.

She's been very helpful and insisted I speak with you. I'm not sure what you think can be done at this point, but I'm willing to tell you what I know.

That's grand! Can you start with telling me what happened? How did you die?

I think I was strangled, but after I blacked out, it's hard to say. Riley's brows furrowed.

And did you see who did this to you?

I know who did this to me — that bleeding melter who wouldn't leave me alone on the Milford Track!

"*I knew it! But when? He's got a strong alibi for the days after your hike.*

I don't know about that. I left Queenstown and headed back up to Christchurch. I was to fly out of Christchurch and took a few days to see this area first. He must have followed me because he accosted me when I was getting some cash from an ATM. He said he had a knife, but I never saw one. He threatened me and told me to take out all the cash I could. Then he made me send a text to my sister asking for more. He got in my car with me, and we drove to a hut — very primitive — no amenities, if you know what I mean.

Was that where you died?

Eventually. We were there a few nights then he left me there and went back to Christchurch to pick up the money from Síofra. He had me sign a note authorising him to pick it up and he took my ID with him. Then he left, locking me in.

I had a gag over my mouth so I couldn't yell, but I stomped the floor for what seemed like hours, but no one heard me.

I don't understand. From what we've learned from the Extreme Hikes folks, he was attracted to you, not wanting to hurt you. Was this about robbery?

He promised me that once he got all the money, he'd let me go. But I don't think it was about the money. He kept going on about teaching me a lesson, making me pay, putting me in my place. I believe he was just really, really angry that I'd had the nerve to turn him down, and to do it so publicly.

Do you know his name?

On the hike he introduced himself as Dan. I never learned anything more than that — didn't want to know.

This hut … any idea where it is located?

Not exactly. We drove south from Christchurch for at least a half-hour. Once out of town he blindfolded me, and he drove the rest of the way. When we stopped, he removed the blindfold. As far as I could tell, we were in the middle of nowhere, hills and scrub brush. We left the car on the side of the road and hiked up a steep hill for about ten minutes. Sorry I can't tell you more.

You've helped a great deal. I understand you don't harbour any feelings of anger or resentment, but it's important that someone like this is held accountable and not allowed to continue to prey on other women. Besides, your sister needs closure and to know your attacker isn't allowed to roam free, unpunished.

My sister! How is Síofra? I'm sorry to cause her pain.

You didn't cause the pain, that's squarely on Daniel Hobson. And she's happy to know you are happy and moving on.

It is a grand place here on the Otherside! Who knew? Tell her I'm looking forward to seeing her again sometime on this side.

With that, Riley looked at Brigid, who nodded slightly, then the two of them dematerialised.

Chapter 20

Is minic ciúin ciontach.
The quiet ones are often guilty.

—Irish Proverb

"I know who killed Riley!" Moira said as she burst through the door of the hotel room.

"Daniel Hobson," Deirdre said.

"Dan — but how do you know that?" Moira deflated.

"A bit of detective work and subterfuge," Deirdre said.

"It doesn't matter who found what; what matters is what do we do about it?" Síofra interjected.

"We can't go to the police with the evidence I've got. I don't think they'll take us seriously if we tell Sergeant Lee that the deceased told us," Moira said.

"You saw Riley? How is she? Did she give you any message for me?" Síofra asked.

Moira relayed her conversation with Riley. When

she got to the part where Dan/Daniel blindfolded Riley and drove the car, Deirdre interrupted.

"What did he do with the car? It was a rental, right? Do we know what car company she used?"

Síofra rummaged in her bag and pulled out a manila envelope. "Inspector Keating gave me these copies of the paperwork she got. There's one of Riley's bank statements with credit card purchases." She handed the pages to Moira.

Moira scanned the list and said, "Here's one for Economic Car Rental. Charged on September twenty-sixth. They post it to your card as soon as you turn it in, right?"

"I believe so. They take the card number up front and charge it at the end. At least that's what they just told me at the rental car company we used," Deirdre said.

"We'll ask the police to check for CCTV footage. It was probably just a drop off — no customer contact — but we could verify that Riley didn't turn it in," Moira said.

"Did she say what he did to her? How did she die?" Síofra said, her voice catching in her throat.

"He choked her, then she blacked out. She's not sure what happened after that, as she soon found herself on the Otherside," Moira said.

"What about this hut? Can we try to find it? See if there's any trace of them being there?" Síofra asked.

Deirdre had made copies of local maps at the

library. She pulled out the one of Christchurch and the surrounding area. "Here's Hornby where Daniel lives. Thirty minutes straight south of Christchurch would put them at Teddington. If they turned east, they'd be following the bay. There's no south road until you get to Purau. Seven kilometres south of Purau — see how the road zigzags here? — is the Monument Track. It's my guess that is where he took her."

"Do we go there tomorrow, or do we take this to the police?" Síofra asked.

"I'd like to pay a visit to the scenic village of Hornby, myself," Deirdre said.

"You think that's wise, to confront a murderer?" Moira asked.

"I just want to get a look at the bloke. Assess him up close. We'll come up with some spiel to give him for our being there …"

"Let's decide in the morning. Right now, I need some sleep in an actual bed and not a chair — even if it was a first-class chair!" Moira said.

The following morning it was decided — well, Deirdre convinced Moira and Síofra — to do a drive-by at the address for Daniel Hobson on their way to the track where they hoped to find evidence that Riley had been there.

"We're just driving by, not stopping or trying to confront him, right?" Moira asked as they drove towards Hornby.

Deirdre didn't answer, but instead pulled into a small corner store. "I have an idea. Won't be long." She jumped out of the car and ran into the store, leaving Moira and Síofra to wonder what was up. She was back in five minutes with a bag of items, which she handed to Moira.

"Cleaning spray, dust rags, a caddy … what's all this?" Moira asked her sister.

"We'll pose as a new cleaning business, going door-to-door for customers — window washers!"

"Sorry? That's chancing your arm! If this is truly the home of Riley's murderer, that's too dangerous," Moira protested.

"He's not going to murder us on his doorstep. Don't you want to get a look at him? The chances of him being outside on his front porch as we drive by are slim."

"I agree with Deirdre. I want to see this gobshite," Síofra added.

"Fine," Moira said.

Ten minutes later they were weaving their way through the suburb of Hornby. The address Deirdre had was on the west side in a relatively new community of modest single-family homes. They drove by the address and parked a few doors down.

"Now what?" Moira asked.

"We knock on the door. Here, let me put these cleaning supplies into the caddy — the perfect prop!" Deirdre's enthusiasm was contagious, and Moira felt butterflies in her stomach as they were about to enter the unknown.

Approaching the house, Moira noticed a curtain move on the front bay window. There was someone home. Someone who saw them coming. The door was opened before they could knock.

"May I help you, ladies?" a man in his mid-thirties, receding hairline of straight brown hair cut short, stood before them. Their eyes were drawn to the long scratch along his cheek and a curved cut that was beginning to scab over on the bridge of his nose.

Moira looked to Deirdre, who began her speech. "We've started up a cleaning business and were wondering if you could use some assistance with washing windows, dusting, that sort of thing."

"I'm afraid not, sorry." He began to close the door, then paused before saying, "I recognise that accent — Irish?"

"We moved here recently from Dublin; good ear on

you! You must have heard plenty of Irish speakers to be so sharp!" Deirdre replied.

"Actually, I've had the recent acquaintance of a young woman of Irish nationality." His stare caused Moira to involuntarily shudder. "Umm. I don't need cleaning, but I have a shed out back that needs tidying, organizing you know, that sort of thing. If you're interested in earning a few dollars …"

"Not really —" Moira began as Síofra said, "Certainly!"

"Maybe we could just take a look at the project and decide, er … Mister …?" Deirdre asked.

"Hobson. Daniel Hobson. And you are …?"

"Deirdre. And this is Moira and Síofra."

"Very Irish names, indeed! Right this way, through the kitchen to the backyard."

The three followed him as he led them to the outside where they saw a small outbuilding, like a potting shed.

"It's dusty and cluttered and I keep thinking I'll get to it but name your price for the job and it's yours," he said with a flourish as he opened the shed door. The women walked into the shed and were immediately confused, for the inside was bare; not so much as a garden rake occupied the space. They turned around in time to see Hobson shut the door behind him, barring the exit and holding a length of lead pipe.

"Now, ladies, tell me what you are really doing here?"

Chapter 21

Aithnítear cara i gcruatan.
It is in hardship that a friend is recognised.

—Irish Proverb

"What do you think you're doing? Let us out of here at once!" Moira shouted.

"You're obviously not cleaning ladies. I recognised you right away from a photo on your sister's phone," he said, indicating Síofra. "How did you find me?"

"Riley told us about you," Moira said. "We are here to make sure you are held accountable for her death."

"Her death? What makes you think she's dead? No one's found a body, as far as I know, and I've been cleared by the police. I have an alibi," he said with a smirk.

"Then tell us how you got those injuries to your face," Síofra said."

"I was hiking. That's where I met your sister. A branch hit me in the face."

"A 'branch' named Riley, I think," Síofra scoffed. "When we do find her body, your DNA will be under her fingernails, for sure!"

"You three are going to wait here, and I am going to call the police and have you arrested for trespassing and harassment. It will be your word against mine, and under the law I have the right to protect my property from trespassers with 'reasonable force.'"

Hobson left and they heard the click of a lock on the door.

"Well, that went well," Deirdre said.

"I hope he does call the police. Then we can tell them what we know — have *them* check that track for the hut where he kept her," Síofra said.

"What exactly can we tell the police that doesn't involve witnesses from the Otherside?" Deirdre asked.

"We can have them check the rental car. Even if they don't have cameras that caught him returning the car, maybe his DNA is in there," Moira suggested.

"And there's the cut on his nose. I can tell by the impression it made that Riley must have hit him with her kubotan," Síofra said.

"Kubotan? What is that?" Moira asked.

In response, Síofra reached into her pocket and pulled out a rounded stick about twelve centimetres in length, smooth with a flattened circular tip at each end.

"This," she said. "Our da got each of us one for Christmas about four years ago, right before he passed. He made us promise we would first, learn how to use it, and second, always keep it handy."

"It doesn't look very intimidating. How does it work?" Moira asked.

"It can be quite lethal. If you hit someone in the right place straight on with the tip, it can break bones, incapacitate, or even kill. That's why I had to check a bag on the plane. I didn't want to take the chance of it getting confiscated."

"Do you think he's really calling the police? Maybe we should call Sergeant Lee and explain our side of it first. For all we know, Hobson is about to get rid of us like he did Riley!" Deirdre said.

Síofra made the call and within twenty minutes, with still no sign of Hobson, a police officer had broken down the door of the shed. Behind the officer stood Sergeant Lee.

"What were you thinking? This could have ended very badly," he said.

"Where is Mr Hobson? Did he call the police as well and tell you we were trespassers?" Deirdre asked.

"There is no sign of him anywhere in the house, and no, we received no calls of trespassing. Another officer is making a thorough check of the premises, but it appears Daniel Hobson has done a runner."

The second officer came out the back door and handed Sergeant Lee a mobile phone in a plastic bag. "Found this in a box under the bed along with a flowered scarf. You said to look for anything suspicious, and a phone and a woman's scarf under a bed seemed suspicious to me …"

"That looks like Riley's phone!" Síofra pulled her phone out of her pocket and held it out. "See? They are the same. We bought them at the same time."

"Let's get you out of here. I want you three down at the station so we can suss out what is going on."

"But —" Moira began, but stopped herself.

"But what?" Sergeant Lee asked.

"Nothing. We were just headed out to —"

"We'll head to the station straightaway, sir!" Deirdre said.

Back in the car, Deirdre explained. "We don't know where Hobson is headed. If we go to the track and check out the hut, we may run into him again. Now that he knows we are on to him, he might have gone straight there to be sure he left no evidence."

"All the more reason we should try to get there first before he destroys evidence!" Síofra said.

"We can't risk it. I'm afraid we must leave this to the

police. With Riley's mobile showing up here, they should be pursuing him more intently now."

Síofra sighed. "We were so close! I'm sure he was about to confess!"

"And if he did, he'd have all the more motive to silence us!" Dierdre reasoned.

"You're right, I know. I appreciate all you're doing for me. You are risking your lives, and I certainly wouldn't have gotten this far without you."

They arrived at the police station and were ushered into Sergeant Lee's office. He arrived soon after.

"Now tell me, why on earth did you go to Daniel Hobson's home?" he asked.

"We had reason to believe he knew more about Riley's disappearance than what he said to the police."

"What reason would that be?"

"We can't divulge our sources at this time," Deirdre said.

"So that's how it is? Two can play at that. It just so happens I've come into some information that caused us to suspect Mr Hobson as well, but I don't have to share that with you either."

"That's just childish! What did you learn?" Síofra demanded.

Sergeant Lee laughed. "Alright, I hope what I tell you

will help you to trust me with what you know. I can see that you will not leave the investigating to us — something your Inspector Keating warned me about — and I think we will all be better off if we try to work together. We got a hit on his name in the system when he applied for a new driver's ID. He reported it stolen on the nineteenth, but that was the day before he checked into the hiking centre for the Grand Tramp. We sent his photo down to Extreme Hikes and they verified that he checked in for the Milford Track, but it now appears that someone else used his identification to check in for the Grand Tramp."

"An accomplice! I knew it! Didn't I say that?" Síofra said, looking at Moira and Deirdre.

"We don't believe it was an accomplice, per se. We questioned a group of housetruckers who camp in the area around Queenstown, and one came forward with the information that he was approached by a gentleman with an offer of one hundred dollars to take his place on the hike. The man said he had important business and didn't want the trip to go to waste. In addition to the money, it meant a week of free food and paid accommodations, so he agreed. The man gave him his ID and said he'd be back at the end of the week to retrieve it, but he hasn't seen him since. He handed over Hobson's ID."

"Housetruckers?" Moira asked.

"Hippies — what you'd call gypsies, I guess. Kiwis who build these traveling houses out of old Bedford trucks or buses and lead a nomadic lifestyle. This one was about the same height and build as Hobson, which is why he was targeted, I guess. The staff member at the hiking centre confessed she hadn't looked closely at the identification. Nothing like that had ever occurred before.

"We were about to bring Mr Hobson back in for questioning when we received your distress call. Now, will you be straight up with me?"

"The rental car," Deirdre began. "There's a charge to Riley's card for returning the car on the twenty-sixth. We believe she was already dead by then, so we were hoping you could check if there is CCTV at the car rental place. It might show who turned in the vehicle."

"We did think of that, and no, there are no cameras where the cars are turned in. The car in question has been loaned out to someone else, but we have left strict instructions to notify us when it is returned. We will go over it very carefully, I assure you." Sergeant Lee paused for a moment, then said, "Why do you believe Riley was dead by the twenty-sixth?"

"I had a dream," Síofra spoke up. "Riley came to me in a dream on the twenty-fourth and asked me to bring her body home."

"Well. Alright, then. Thank you for sharing that with me. Is there anything else?"

Síofra glanced at Moira before continuing. "She said she was in a hut south of Christchurch. Something about a Monument Track?"

"I see. And I'm guessing that is where you will be heading after you leave here?"

When no one responded, he said, "I can't stop you, so I'm sending an officer with you. With Hobson still out there, it could be dangerous for you. Wait here a moment."

He returned shortly with a young man following. "This is Constable Devin. He will drive out to the track, and you are to follow him and do everything he says."

"Thank you! We appreciate your help!" Deirdre exclaimed.

"Wait in your vehicle out front, and I will pull up next to you. Then you can follow me," Constable Devin said.

"Shouldn't you be following us? We have the directions from Riley in Síofra's dream," Deirdre replied.

"I've done my share of tramping. I'm quite familiar with the location of Monument Track," Constable Devin said.

In the privacy of their vehicle, Deirdre turned to Síofra and said, "That was quick thinking to put Riley's message into your dream."

"I figured he'd believe I had a dream more than he'd believe Moira talked with Riley's ghost. He may not have given it much credence, but he believes we believe in it and doesn't want us to go off on our own investigating it. After being locked in Hobson's shed, I'm glad Constable Devin is assigned to help us. I only hope he doesn't look at it as a babysitting assignment."

"He seems quite young, almost a baby himself. I hope he's experienced enough to keep his wits if we do come across Riley's murderer," Moira said.

They followed the police car for over forty minutes, taking the route Deirdre had mapped out the night before using Riley's recollections. When they got to the pull-out near the start of the Track, they pulled in and parked. They were the only two vehicles in the area. Constable Devin got out of his car and came to the driver's window.

"Stay here while I look around," he said.

"No way! We are coming with you," Síofra said, as Moira and Deirdre got out of the car.

"Fine," he said with a sigh. "This track is closed to trampers at this time of year for the lambing season, so you'll need to stay close behind me."

First in line behind the constable, Deirdre noted he had a pistol and a taser on his belt. She wasn't sure if that was worrisome or reassuring. They climbed over a locked gate and started along a barely discernible path in the grassy hillside. Strewn with rocks and tussocks of tall dry grasses, the climb wasn't too steep, but all three women were not used to the exertion and began to slow. It seemed much longer but was close to ten minutes when Constable Devin halted in the shelter of a lone tree, about twenty metres away from the hut. The hut was tiny — less than four metres by two metres — made of red, corrugated metal. It stood on several wooden posts about a half metre off the ground.

Síofra shuddered. "Just thinking about Riley in that place is disturbing," she said.

"Shhhh. He may be inside. There's no window on this side, so stay here while I get closer," Constable Devin said as he began a slow crouch towards the hut.

The women lost sight of him as he turned the corner of the hut, but moments later he re-emerged waving them forward. When they reached him, he said, "The hut is empty, but someone has been here recently, as you can see the dust has been disturbed on the floor. We won't go inside and disturb any evidence, but you can take a squiz from the door."

The all looked at him blankly.

"A squiz, a look," He stepped aside for them to peer in at the bleak interior. Four wooden bunkbeds lined the far wall. A crude table and benches were opposite. There was no heat source, no electricity, no water or toilet facility.

"This hut is rarely used by trampers anymore, so it's possible the footprints are from Hobson and your sister. As I said earlier, this track is closed to trampers from July through October. Whoever was here, was here illegally. We'll have to get the forensics team out if the sergeant thinks it's necessary."

"If he thinks it's necessary? This is where my sister was held captive! She was probably killed here! We need to look around the area; maybe her body is nearby," Síofra said as she began to move away and head towards the rolling hills that ascended towards a higher rock outcropping.

"Wait! Stop! We must stick together! What makes you so sure she was here?" The constable jogged towards Síofra and grabbed her arm, but she shook him off and kept walking.

"Síofra, wait up! He's right — we need to stay together," Deirdre headed after her with Moira right behind.

But as Moira got further away from the hut, a feeling of unease began to grow within her. She stopped and looked back at the lonely little building. Something — *or someone* — was calling to her. When Deirdre noticed Moira wasn't joining them, she tugged at Síofra and indicated her sister. Moira returned to the hut and began circling it.

"Keep away from that bush!" Constable Devin yelled as he ran back towards Moira. She stopped and waited for him to reach her. They were on the side of the hut that contained the lone window, around the corner from the door. When Deirdre and Síofra joined them, he pointed to the large bushy plant that was growing alongside the hut.

"This is Onga-onga. It's a type of stinging nettle. It grows all over the place out here. It's got a neurotoxin in its spines. Brush up against the thorns and it's not just excruciating pain you'll experience. If you've been stung bad enough, you could become paralysed, stop breathing and die. Hmmm. It looks like someone or something — maybe an animal — fell into it. See how it's matted down here —"

"We need to check under the building," Moira interrupted.

"Why —" Constable Devin began, but Moira was already on her hands and knees, then down on her stomach as she peered under the building.

"There's something here!" she called.

"Bugger all! Let me see!"

Moira moved aside and the constable took her place on the ground. "It's a body, alright!" He stood up and took out his mobile.

"Sir, we've found something … yea, nah, *under* the hut. I'm thinking it's the girl … no sign of Hobson … right." He ended the call and turned to the women.

"They're sending a team to retrieve the body. We are to stay put until they arrive."

"Jaysus, Mary and Joseph! Is it my sister?" Síofra got down on the ground, but Constable Devin yanked her up.

"We must leave her until the team arrives. There's nothing you can do for her now."

"I need to see her! Leave me alone!"

"Let her go," Deirdre said calmly. She took Síofra by the hand and together, they knelt by the hut. Looking under, Síofra let out a sob, and Deirdre pulled her away into an embrace. She rocked her back and forth as Síofra wailed.

Leaving Deirdre to comfort Síofra, Constable Devin approached Moira.

"What made you look under there? Did you know what you would find?"

"Call it a hunch?" She posed it as a question and the constable raised an eyebrow.

"Okay, here goes. You're going to think I'm balmy, but I have a connection with the dead. In this instance, I sensed … something, I can't explain it. I'm sorry. It was like Riley's spirit was directing me to look under the house."

"Yea, nah … I'm not putting that in my report. Let's go with the 'hunch.'"

Deirdre manoeuvred Síofra to a grouping of rocks some ways away from the hut where she, Síofra and Moira sat and talked quietly while they waited.

"You alright?" Deirdre asked as she twirled a lock of hair around her finger.

"I don't know what happened. I knew she was dead. I believed that Moira saw and talked with her spirit. It's just … actually seeing her body lying there in the dirt, abandoned and … *dead* … it made it all too real."

"Just focus on the fact that she really is in a better place and is happy," Moira said.

"I know, I know. I'm trying …"

It took a little over an hour before the forensics team and coroner arrived. Moira, Deirdre and Síofra continued to watch the activity from their rocky seats, with Síofra occasionally rising to pace and wring her hands.

When they got Riley's body out from under the hut and laid out on a tarp, Síofra rushed over but was held back by a Māori female member of the forensics team.

"My deepest empathy to you for your loss, ma'am, but you mustn't touch her, not until she's been thoroughly examined."

"Come, Síofra. Let's go for a walk," Deirdre said.

"Don't go far," Constable Devin said. "I'm still responsible for you and you are not to go out of my sight. And keep away from the Monument; the rock there is unstable since last year's earthquake."

The three women started along the track that led from the hut through the pastureland towards the Monument — the seven-hundred-metre-high hill looming ahead of them that gave the track its name. Even if they'd wanted to defy Constable Devin and hike up its slope, they weren't wearing the proper foot gear to even attempt it. They hadn't anticipated this type of activity when they packed and were all three wearing runners, which were now muddy and soaked through to their stockings.

They came upon another cluster of rocks and Síofra chose the largest to sit upon. "I'm just so exhausted! I think it's the letdown of finding Riley. I've nothing now to look forward to except getting her home."

"There's still the matter of finding her killer and bringing him to justice," Deirdre said.

"I can understand Riley's thinking somewhat — punishing him won't bring her back," Síofra replied.

"But he's still a danger to others. He can't be allowed to get away with murder," Moira added.

Deirdre still had too much energy to sit, and circled the rock cluster, kicking at stones and picking up a few to chuck at a tree not far distant. Rounding a large boulder, she stopped and let out a cry. There before her, lying on the ground and staring up at her through dead eyes was the body of Daniel Hobson.

Chapter 22

Ní mar a shíltear a bhítear.
Things are not always as they seem.

—Irish Proverb

"Constable Devin! Come quickly! We've found Daniel Hobson!" Moira was running full tilt down the path back to the hut, leaving Deirdre and Síofra to remain with the body of Riley's killer.

"What? Where?"

Hands on her knees and head bowed to catch her breath after her sprint, Moira got out, "He's dead. Up the path."

The constable didn't wait for her to collect herself enough to accompany him, but took off along the path he'd watched the three women walk a short time ago.

"Over here!" Deirdre called when she saw Constable Devin bounding up the path. He joined her and Síofra who were both still staring dumbfoundedly at the body at their feet.

"What do you think happened to him?"

"That remains to be seen. You ladies head back to the hut and tell the forensics lead that we'll be returning with two bodies."

It took three days before they heard back from Sergeant Lee. They spent the weekend resting and surfing through the local television channels with an occasional walk through the Botanical Gardens. They just weren't ready for any normal sight-seeing activities beyond that. Deirdre returned to the library and sent an email to Bronagh and Nuala letting them know what had transpired over the past few days. When Sergeant Lee called Monday morning, they were ready to wrap up their time in this land Down Under. He said he would meet them at Christchurch Hospital at one o'clock that afternoon.

"May I see her now?" Síofra asked.

"At one o'clock."

Moira and Deirdre accompanied Síofra as she navigated the floors, elevators and hallways of the city hospital to the basement where the morgue was located.

Sergeant Lee was waiting for them outside the door.

"I'm so sorry for your loss. You have my deepest empathy." He bowed slightly then opened the door and ushered them into the office space of the department. "Wait here a moment, and I'll make sure all is ready for you."

He returned with a woman in a lab coat, eyeglasses perched on top of her head and a clipboard in hand. The women recognised her as one of the team that had extricated Riley out from under the hut.

"This is Doctor Campbell, our coroner. She has performed the postmortem on your sister. She can answer any questions you may have."

"I saw you at the hut when they took away Riley," Síofra said.

"Yes. I am so sorry for your loss. Are you ready?"

"I am." Turning to Moira and Deirdre, Síofra said, "Come with me, please?"

"Whatever you need," Deirdre said.

Riley's body lay on the stainless-steel table with a white sheet covering her from head to toe. Doctor Campbell took hold of the sheet and glancing at Síofra, who nodded slightly, pulled it gently away from the head, revealing Riley's face. Síofra bit her lip but moved next to the doctor and gazed down at her sister.

"How did she die?"

"Strangulation."

"Did she suffer? Where there other marks of … torture that you found?"

"No."

"Was she … did he …?" Síofra couldn't bring herself to vocalise the unmentionable horror.

"There were no signs of sexual assault, but the DNA match of his skin and blood under Riley's fingernails has provided us with enough physical evidence to identify her assailant."

"I knew it! She did give him those scratches and cuts on his face! Are you also the one who examined Daniel Hobson?"

"I am, but I am not at liberty to share those findings with you. You'll have to speak with Sergeant Lee about that. My deepest empathy to you and your whānau. Would you like any more time with your sister?"

Síofra smoothed a lock of hair from Riley's face, touched her fingers to her lips and placed them on Riley's forehead.

"Slán go fóill, a stór."

They rejoined Sergeant Lee in the outer office.

"As you have requested, Riley's remains will be shipped to Dublin for burial. Is there anything else I can do for you, Ms O'Cleary?"

"I would like to know what you've learned about Daniel Hobson," Síofra said.

"Ah, of course you do. It has been determined that he died of acute acetylcholine poisoning, which occurred when he came into contact with Urtica ferox, or the Ongaonga plant. It caused his muscles to weaken and become paralyzed, his breathing to be constricted, blindness soon followed and ultimately, death."

"A fitting end. And you have the evidence needed to confirm he is Riley's murderer?"

"His DNA matches what was found in the samples taken from under her fingernails as well as what we got from her rental car — it had been wiped down, but no one ever completely obliterates everything. We got his print from the lever to move the driver's seat back. So, yes, we have our killer. You may be interested to know we are now cross-referencing his DNA — the first time it has been in our system — with other assaults and murders over the years. It's quite possible we could solve a lot more cold cases."

"That would be a great benefit from this whole affair. Thank you, Sergeant. I can go home now."

Once back at the hotel, the mood was subdued but relieved.

"Our tickets are Tuesday to Tuesday; are we ready to head home tomorrow? Or do you need more time?"

Deirdre asked. "Riley's body won't be flown back to Dublin until Thursday; we might be able to get on the same flight."

"I don't think so. I'm ready to leave tomorrow. I'll plan on meeting her plane when she arrives."

"I could use one more alone-time in the Gardens before we leave, if you won't miss me for an hour or so," Moira said. "I could pick up some Chinese takeaway on my way back for dinner. There's that Asian restaurant near the Gardens."

"Sounds grand! Take your time and we'll be here when you get back," Deirdre said.

As Moira approached the seating area she'd gone to when she made contact with Riley and Nana Brigid, she began formulating the questions she had that were still unsettling her mind. No stranger to supposed 'coincidences,' or 'happy little accidents,' she couldn't let go of the poetic justice of Hobson dying by asphyxiation, so similar to the way he had dispatched Riley. Could there have been some assistance from the Otherside? She wasn't sure if she should attempt to reach out to her grandmother, or to Riley, so once she was seated, she just quieted her mind and opened her heart to whatever would come.

I've been watching you come and go over the last few days with my sister and yours. I've wanted to talk to you, but knew it had to be when you were alone. I'm so glad you've come!

Riley seemed to be glowing a little more than when she first appeared last week.

Riley! You must know why I am here, then.

Riley laughed. *I believe I do — which is why I am here on my own. Brigid said she wanted no part in this.*

I see. So, tell me, did you help Daniel Hobson along to the Otherside?

He seemed to be in a hurry. I watched him lock you in the shed, but I knew you'd be okay there if he was on the move, so I followed him. When he went back to that hut, I was curious, but then I got miffed when he started manhandling my body again, trying to get me out of the hut and shoving me very roughly, I might add, under the building. I may still be learning about how things work here, but I think I've got the basics down, and there might have been a pretty strong wind that came up suddenly just as he straightened up from coming out from under the hut. When he lost his balance, I didn't see any reason to intervene to help him out, would you?

Anyway, he thrashed around a bit and got good and stung in that lovely bush. When he finally got up, I think he was pretty horrified, like he knew what was going to happen. He kept saying, 'no! no! no!' until he couldn't say anything anymore. He was disoriented and had a hard time walking, but he made it to those rocks where you found him before he collapsed. I didn't stick around after that. I'm sure they sent someone appropriate to meet him. I haven't seen him here on this side, but then, I understand his kind go to a different area apart from the regulars.

Thank you for telling me. I thought it was too neatly done. You may be interested to know that the police are looking into him as the suspect in several unsolved murders here, now that they've got his DNA.

Oh, I already know about that. I've met up with three women here already who had similar encounters with our Mr Hobson. I'm glad he's finally off where he can't hurt anyone else. Will you tell my sister I love her? Thank you all for coming here to bring me home!

Riley didn't wait for Moira to answer but faded away with a wave and a smile.

BURIED SECRETS

Chapter 23

—

Ná tabhair breith ar an chéad scéal.
Never judge on first opinions.

—Irish Proverb

November 2012

"Nuala! This is your ma. Call me back, I have a fun little project for you! Byebyebyebyebyebye …"

Nuala had been out riding Mahogany, the newest addition to their stud farm. Although *Bonnie Mahogany, King of the Curragh* had come to them in the Spring of that year, it had taken several months of daily attending to the feisty stallion, wooing him with soft words and carrots, before he would even allow her to put a saddle on him. Despite the chilly weather she never could turn down an opportunity to ride this beauty. It was a momentary burst of exhilaration and freedom for both as they raced across the fields, her chestnut waves and his almost black mane whipping in the wind.

When she returned to the house and was able to check her messages, she immediately called Dymphna back.

"Howsagoin', Ma? What's the craic?"

"You busy? I don't want to bother you if you're busy."

"Just got in from riding, Ma. I wouldn't have called you back if I was too busy to talk!"

"But how's your workload? Are you able to take on a small genealogy project?"

"I have a catering affair at the end of the month, but I'm free for a few days. What's the project and why don't you do it?"

"It has a bit of a … well … let's just say it's more of a job for the Gallagher Investigators …"

"Really? There's a bit of the supernatural to it?"

"Not yet. But it's a tough case — not many records available. Let me tell you how it began. A nice couple is here for a few days at the inn. The other morning, I was in the office working on some family history when Cecilia — that's the woman of the couple — popped in and asked for advice on places to see in the area. I told her I'd finish up with this family group sheet I was working on and then be right with her.

"Then she asked, 'what's a family group sheet?' Well, you know me once that door was opened. I'm afraid I unloaded on her about the virtues and joys of family history work. After a half-hour or so, I thought I'd bored her to death, but she was still really interested. Then she asked me to help her with finding her own family history.

"Nuala, mo chroí, what I would really like is for Cecilia to tell you her tale herself. I told her you might be a better resource for her. She and Eamon — that's her husband — are off to the Fastnet Lighthouse but plan to be back here at the inn this evening. Can I have her give you a call?"

"That would be grand, Ma. Is everything else going okay?"

"Busy, busy! When will I be seeing you down this way?"

"Not sure. Probably not before Christmas, but we'll definitely be there then!"

"That would be grand! Tabhair aire, bye-bye, bye-bye!" Slán, Ma!"

The call came through just as Seán and Nuala were cleaning up after dinner. Nuala took it in the library, her favourite room in the house. The dark wood panelling and floor-to-ceiling shelves of leather-bound books gave the room an air of sophistication, while the plush comfy chairs, warm lighting and hand-knotted oriental rugs provided a cosy, comfortable feel.

With pen and paper at the ready, she took the call.

"This is Nuala Kennedy."

"Nuala! Cecilia Higgins here! Your ma suggested I call you for some family history help."

"Ma said you are having difficulty finding records?"

"That's putting it mildly. It's really about my mother — my birth mother, that is. I was in foster care for all my formative years. The only thing I've been able to learn (when I was a teenager from a foster mum who was not happy with me when I had a messy room) is that I was of illegitimate birth and I'll probably end up like my ma, a laundress in the Magdalene Laundries."

Chapter 24

Ar scáth a chéile a mhaireann na daoine
People live in one another's shadow.

—Irish Proverb

There was quiet on the line for a moment while Nuala tried to form a response. Then she said, "I'm sorry, I've heard about the Magdalenes, of course, but I equated it with another time in the past. If you don't mind my asking, when were you born?"

"Not many people know the details about the Magdalenes, but I've recently joined a group of its victims that is trying to get it more into the public consciousness — to try to get the records opened so victims like me can learn about our past.

"I was born in 1955. I just turned fifty-seven last August. The laundries operated from 1922 to 1996."

"That means your mother may still be alive!"

"Most women went in when they were in their early twenties, but there are known to have been some as young as fourteen, so I suppose it is possible my mother could be in her eighties now."

"Ma mentioned that the records weren't available. You're saying there are records, they are just sealed?"

"That's right. The Catholic nuns have so far refused to open their records to the public. The general idea is that these homes run by the nuns were places where 'morally corrupt' women were sent — you know, prostitutes — but through this network I've learned about, it appears there were several routes to these facilities. If a woman had a child out of wedlock, she was no longer fit for society. Even if she were raped or the victim of incest, that didn't matter. Some were put there by their own families if they had disgraced them in any way. Even for the crime of being 'too pretty' and thus at 'moral risk.'"

"That's outrageous! I didn't realise that," Nuala said.

"It gets worse. If a woman was carrying an illegitimate child, her path led first through one of the many mother and baby homes in the country."

"Can you tell me more about those?"

"They were also run by the nuns. They took in unwed mothers and once the baby was born — if it was born alive, that is, since for a long time the nuns tried to deal with the births themselves and didn't call in doctors or midwives to assist, thus leading to high infant mortality rates — they separated mother and baby. The healthy children were adopted out, often sold to wealthy American couples or put in what we now call foster care, but it was highly unregulated. A third choice was an industrial school. The mothers were then sent to the laundries."

"I've heard of the industrial schools. They aren't still around though, right?"

"Well, the name has been changed, they are now called Children Detention Schools to house and school neglected, orphaned, and abandoned children, but they are basically the same thing."

"And you don't know how your mother ended up in a Magdalene laundry?"

"I don't even know my mother's name. There is a name on my birth certificate, but I learned that often the nuns would change the 'penitents' names, to give them a fresh start, to forget their past. I was just hoping my birth date and place would be a good starting point, but I don't have any experience with doing family history. When I talked to Dymphna about it, she said you and your sisters have a business that might be able to help me."

"To be honest with you, we have a better chance of getting the information you seek if your mother is deceased then if she is still alive," Nuala said, not sure how much more than that she wanted to share.

"I don't understand," Cecelia said.

"Let's just say our sources are highly unusual. I'll need to talk to my sisters about your case before I can even tell you we can accept it, let alone help in any way. Can I call you back in a few days?"

"Of course. We live in Roscommon but will be on holiday in Schull for another few days. I appreciate any help you can give."

"Is there anything else you can tell me that may help our inquiries?" Nuala asked.

"If you give me your email, I'll send you the information that is on my birth certificate, and anything else I can remember."

Nuala gave her the email address for Gallagher Investigations so it would be available to all three sisters, then the two said their goodbyes. After ending the call, Nuala immediately called Moira and filled her in on Cecelia's case.

"I know a bit about the Magdalenes. There was a film shown on the telly about the whole thing last year. I believe it was called *The Forgotten Maggies* — such a disgrace, what was done to those women! Deirdre's right here —you're on speaker — and she is nodding. Call Cecelia and offer our services. We'll do our best to help."

"Check the business email. Cecilia has sent some information for us to review, then I'll call her back."

Deirdre opened the email and read aloud:

"'Greetings! Thank you for considering my case. Your ma sings your praises, and I know you will be my best recourse to finding out about my mother. Attached is a photocopy of my birth record. Let me know if you have any questions, go raibh maith agat, Cecilia.'"

She then opened the document attached. It read:

Cecilia Carmody, born August 10, 1955, at St. Gerald's Mother and Baby Home, Dublin, Eire.
Mother: Anne Carmody, Father: Unknown

"Cecilia was right — not much information to go on here, but the mother's name is listed, we just aren't sure if it's her real name, correct?" Moira commented.

"That's right," Nuala replied.

"I'm getting a strong feeling that we need to take this case. If her mother is alive, we will find her. If she isn't, we may hear from her. Either way, we can help," Moira said.

"That's grand! I'll call Cecilia back and tell her we're on it," Nuala said.

Chapter 25

Is binn béal ina thost.
Silence is golden.

—Irish Proverb

Nuala tossed and turned in her bed and soon found herself being yanked out of a vehicle by a rough hand and marched to the front of a tall, brick building. The wooden door creaked open on unoiled hinges to reveal a dark hallway and a woman in nun's habit ready to take her in the hand-off. She couldn't get a glimpse of the man who brought her here, but she felt like she should know him. The door shut behind her and the woman, leaving the man on the outside.

She felt suffocated, cold, the damp seeping into her bones. The nun, for that's what she must be, hustled her up a long flight of stairs and into a dormitory of beds lining the two walls with a walkway between. It was early evening, but the beds were all occupied, young girls like herself sitting upright on their assigned beds. She was brought to stand before one unoccupied bed and was told to strip and put on the grey shift that lay upon the thin sheet.

"But —" she began.

"Silence! You are not to speak unless spoken to. Ever. Not even in whispers to these others," the nun said, waving her hand vaguely at the other inmates.

And inmates they were, as this was as close to or worse than any prison.

In an instant, the dream morphed to another scene: breakfast of one slice of bread and a cup of water. Then she found herself marching single file with the other girls to another damp room filled with sinks, and tables piled high with linens: bloody linens from hospitals, foul prison garb, yards and yards of sheets. It felt like hours, even in her dream, that she scrubbed item after item on a scrub board until her knuckles were raw and bleeding. She started to sob, but a ruler came crashing down on her shoulders with a command of 'Silence!'

Nuala woke with a shudder. A sob escaped her lips, and she shook with a feeling of dread and hopelessness. But there was Seán, snoring softly beside her, the light of a near-full moon coming in through the mullioned windows. She was home — Hawthorn House — where she and Seán were building a life together. But the dream seemed so real she still couldn't shake it. *Whatever that was, it really happened to someone.* And the more she thought on it, the more she got the feeling that *someone* was asking for her help.

CHAPTER 26

Beidh lá eile ag an bPaorach.
Power will have another day.

—Irish Proverb

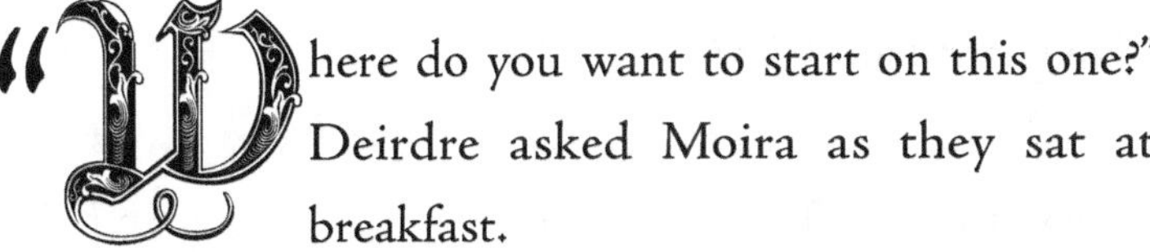

"Where do you want to start on this one?" Deirdre asked Moira as they sat at breakfast.

"I think we need to talk to Cecilia again and see what she has already done to try to find her mother. There's no sense in reinventing the wheel."

"Agreed. Shall I call her now?"

"No time like the present!"

Deirdre made the call.

"Dia dhuit."

"Dia is Muire dhuit, Cecilia, this is Deirdre Gallagher. Do you have a moment to answer a few questions?"

"I'm so pleased you called! I just spoke with Nuala

who said you have accepted my case. What can I tell you?"

"What have you already done to search for your mother?"

"As I mentioned to Nuala, I joined a group called Justice for Magdalenes —or JFM — which is an advocacy group dedicated to getting justice for the victims of the Magdalene Laundry scheme. They petitioned the state for an apology and redress for the treatment of those institutionalised in the laundries as well as their children. So far, the petitions have been refused."

"Have you approached the Sisters of Our Lady of Hope who ran the mother and baby homes and the Magdalene laundries?"

"They refuse to even respond or speak to any of our representatives. Two years ago, the JFM petitioned the IHRC — the Irish Human Rights Commission — and they agreed the matter needed looking into. That's as far as it went, though. Then last year the JFM petitioned the UCAT — UN Committee Against Torture. That resulted in the UN committee recommendation to the Irish State that a full investigation be conducted. We're waiting to hear where that goes."

"What about cemetery records, are those available to the public?" Moira prompted.

"The JFM are working on compiling lists of those

who died and have found most laundry victims are buried in Glasnevin Cemetery, some in Donnybrook and a few in a small cemetery on the property of St. Mary Magdalen's convent. Most of the burials were in communal graves with no individual markers. Which is why we need the Sisters of Our Lady of Hope to open their records. If names of the deceased were recorded at all, it was their first name only and the first initial of their last name. Oh! It seems so hopeless!"

"It sounds like you and your group have done a lot already; we don't need to duplicate those efforts. We'll work on things on our end and let you know what we discover. Don't lose hope!" Deirdre said.

After hanging up, Deirdre turned to her sister and asked, "Are you ready now to ask some questions of the dead?"

"Not yet. I'm not convinced that Cecilia's mother is dead. I'd like to check at the care centres where the Magdalenes who were still living were sent when the laundries closed in 1996. It sounds like these women remained in the care of the nuns even after the laundries were closed down. Where else could they go if they had no relatives to take them in, no money, no livelihood to sustain themselves?" Moira reasoned.

"Good point. I'll do some research on where the survivors were relocated after the closures," Deirdre said.

Deirdre's research revealed that there were three homes in the area, all run by the Sisters of our Lady of Hope. One was called Saint Martha's Nursing Centre, one was the Frederick Street Centre, and the third was called the Respite Home on Carnlough Rd, not far from Glasnevin Cemetery. There were a few others in Cork and Kilkenny, but they decided to focus on the Dublin area. They made appointments to visit the Frederick Street Centre and the Carnlough Respite Home the following day.

When they arrived at Frederick Street, they were met by the Mother Superior, Sister Richael.

"Welcome to our Home for the aged and infirm. How may I help you today?" Sister Richael said.

"We are looking for a woman who was once a Magdalene in a laundry here in Dublin," Deirdre began.

"I see. Come in. We can discuss this in my office."

She turned and they followed her inside, through a corridor with highly polished wood floors and colourful icons of Irish saints on the walls. Entering through a door about halfway down the hall, she indicated several chairs for the two sisters.

"Now, tell me, who exactly are you looking for?"

"Her name on her daughter's birth record is Anne Carmody." Deirdre held out the photocopy of Cecilia's birth certificate for the nun to view.

"I can tell you that no one by that name is here in this facility," Sister Richael said.

"She may have another name. We understand that often the names of the women on the birth records of their illegitimate children were changed or disguised. Do you have any cross-referencing documents that could help us learn Anne's actual name?" Moira asked.

"Am I to understand that you are representing someone? This Anne Carmody is not related to either of you?"

"That's correct. We are representing Cecilia Higgins born Carmody," Deirdre replied.

"We are a small group here. There are only fifteen women who have been here for more than a few years. I can vouch for each of them, knowing their history, that none are or ever were known by the name Anne Carmody. And none have ever given birth."

"Well, thank you for your time. We won't take up more of it." Deirdre stood up, as did Moira. Sister Richael put out her hand and the women shook it.

"I'm sorry I couldn't be of more assistance. Good luck in your search," she said, leading them to the door.

Back in the Mini Cooper, Moira asked her sister, "Do you think she is sincere? She seemed nice enough."

"I didn't detect any falseness to her. She didn't hesitate or become flustered by our questions."

"On to appointment number two: Carnlough Road," Moira said, starting up the Mini.

The Carnlough Respite Home was a grander affair, housed in a repurposed hotel. They were escorted to the administrator, a Sister Dana, by a novice who must have taken a vow of silence as she only bowed them in and motioned them to follow her.

Sister Dana seemed in a hurry as she didn't invite them to sit, and she also remained standing during the interview.

"What is this about now?" she asked.

Deirdre handed her the birth certificate and explained their errand.

"I'm sorry, there is no one here of that description. All the women here are from good homes who have voluntarily entered Holy Orders. They have taken vows of chastity and poverty and have been in the service of our Lord all their lives. I really can't help you further. Go n-éirí leat." She rang a little bell on her desk and the novice re-entered the room to escort them out.

Their appointment at Saint Martha's Nursing Centre

wasn't until the following day, so Moira suggested they drive through Glasnevin Cemetery, since they were in that neighbourhood. It was a vast expanse — 124 acres providing the last resting place for hundreds of thousands of the famous and the anonymous.

"I feel like I need to come here for an extended meditation session," Moira said, as the Mini Cooper meandered slowly among the monuments. "There are many unsettled souls here."

"Let's get home and regroup. Are you up for pizza tonight? We can brainstorm our next approach, should this last home prove as unproductive as the others," Deirdre said.

The next morning the sisters pulled into the car park for Saint Martha's Nursing Centre. The building housing the centre was a part of the original laundry which had been refurbished. Deirdre and Moira were met at the door by a nun who appeared to be in her late sixties. She introduced herself as Sister Bernadette, secretary to the Reverend Mother Fachtna. They walked down a hallway and Sister Bernadette knocked quietly on a door that indicated 'Administrator.'

The Reverent Mother stood as they entered the office

and said, 'Welcome, have a seat. That will be all, Sister Bernadette. I am Mother Fachtna, the administrator here. How may I assist you?"

"We are Deirdre and Moira Gallagher, of Gallagher Investigations," Deirdre said, handing the Reverent Mother their business card. "We are here on behalf of a woman whose mother was institutionalised in one of your Magdalene laundries. She is trying to trace her mother's whereabouts, to learn if she might possibly be still alive. We understand that many of the residents of the laundries were moved into care homes following the laundry closures in 1996."

"I see. And you believe this woman may be a resident here?"

"We don't know, but there aren't too many places in Dublin where she could be and this seems the most likely, as we've already checked with the two others in the area with no success," Moira replied. "We have a copy of our client's birth certificate."

Moira placed the copy on the sister's desk. Mother Fachtna glanced briefly at it and said, "It is difficult to nearly impossible to trace these women, as the names on certificates were often misrepresented to protect them. Names of residents were changed upon entering. I don't see how I can help you."

"Would it be possible for us to meet with your current residents and chat with them? Perhaps they may have recollections of the past that would indicate a relationship with our client," Deirdre suggested.

"I'm sorry, but I fear that would be extremely disruptive to our residents. Many are in varying stages of dementia or infirmity. We feel it is best to allow them to live out the rest of their lives in peace and quiet without dredging up the difficulties and hardships of the past." She thanked them, stood and handed back the photocopied birth record to Deirdre. She then called for Sister Bernadette to show them out.

At the door of the home Deirdre turned to Sister Bernadette and asked, "Just how many residents do you have here who were once Magdalenes?"

Not holding out much hope of even getting an answer, she was surprised when the sister replied, "There are about forty women here. At least half of them have been in this or other institutions of the Sisters of Our Lady of Hope their whole lives."

Seizing on this opening and feeling Sister Bernadette might be more sympathetic than her superior, Deirdre continued. "Are you familiar enough with these women to know their history? Is there anyone here who might have had a child born illegitimately in 1955?"

"I don't know. I don't know …" Sister Bernadette was twisting the corner of her habit in her hands as she spoke. "Let me walk you to your car."

They moved away from the building and the nun seemed to visibly relax. "I came to the convent through an industrial school. I know things. It wasn't a good place, but I was able to find peace in the convent. Others have come here looking for their loved ones, to no avail. It's not right. If your client's mother *is* here, they have a right to meet. There may be a way I can help you."

Deirdre gave her one of their business cards. "Please contact us any time. We so appreciate any help you can provide."

Sister Bernadette nodded, took the card and it disappeared into some inner recess of her habit. She turned and walked briskly back to the door.

Chapter 27

—

Uireasa a mhéadaíonn cumha.
Absence makes the heart grow fonder.

—Irish Proverb

Several days went by and they were beginning to think they would not hear from the nun, but then they got a phone call.

"Reverent Mother will be in a meeting all afternoon. Can you come to the centre at half-three today?"

"We will be there."

They had barely parked when Sister Bernadette came out the door and straight to their car. She presented a sheaf of photocopied pages from some sort of notebook and pressed them into Deirdre's hands.

"I'd seen this some time ago; it took me a while to find it and then I had to quickly make copies."

"What am I looking at?" Deirdre asked, scanning

the columns. There were dates running along the first column, a name in the second, a third column labelled 'age at admittance,' a fourth that was headed 'new name/number,' and the last was a wide column indicating who was the referring person or where the candidate had arrived from.

"These are the name changes Mother Fachtna mentioned. This goes back years, but I only copied the pages from the 1940s through the 1960s, as you mentioned the birth occurred within that time." She glanced over her shoulder and said, "I must go. Mother Superior will be returning from her meeting soon."

And with that, she turned and hurried back to the door, her veil swirling around her in the breeze.

Not wanting to be seen by Mother Fachtna in the car park, but not being able to wait until they got home, the sisters pulled into a Tesco lot. As they scanned the pages for Anne Carmody, they found her in the column for the year 1955. She was a transfer into the laundry at age fifteen from St. Cyra Industrial School for Girls in Dublin.

"There's something written in this last column next to St. Cyra. It's faint, hard to read." Deirdre switched on the interior light and held the page up to it. "Ah … I believe it says 'pregnant.'"

"How does a young woman in an industrial school for girls, presumably kept under lock and key and hidden away from the world, as the stories go, become pregnant?" Moira mused.

"Good question. My guess is someone who worked there at the school was the responsible party," Deirdre replied.

"Here it says her name before the transfer was Cara Moore. If we could get the records of the industrial school we might learn when and from where Cara Moore arrived at the school," Moira said.

"We can check when we get home. I wonder if Cecilia's group has any information on that. We should call and check in with her. Give her this information right away."

"Let's go!" Moira said as she started up the Mini Cooper.

When they reached Cecilia, she was thrilled with the progress they'd made. "I can't believe you found someone willing to help you! Can I get copies of those pages? You have no idea how long and hard we've been trying to get that sort of documentation from the Sisters of Our Lady of Hope. That could go a long way to helping more of the survivors."

"I'll get them scanned and emailed to you right away," Deirdre said.

"My mother's actual name was Cara Moore … That

name means nothing to me. I'm not aware of any Moore relatives. Every little titbit of information is like a nugget of gold to me, though. Thank you so much! What will you do now?"

"We wondered if the JFM had any information on the industrial schools. Any documentation made available from them?" Deirdre asked.

"They are as tight-lipped about that as they are about the mother and baby homes and the laundries, I'm afraid."

"Well then, our next step is Moira's Plan B. We'll let you know how that works out," Deirdre said before ringing off.

"Plan B?" Moira asked.

"You know. The communing-with-the-dead Plan B."

"Ah, right." Moira inhaled deeply and let it out slowly. "I guess I'm ready for that. I want to start at Glasnevin, as that was reported as the burial ground for the majority of the Magdalenes. I'm going to get a good night's sleep first, though, and tackle it in the morning."

In the morning, Moira found Deirdre in the kitchen preparing a full Irish for her to be properly fuelled for her visit to the cemetery.

"You never can tell how long it's going to take to make contact, so I thought I'd have you prepared for the long haul," Deirdre said, plating blood pudding, an egg scramble, grilled tomatoes and bubble and squeak from their dinner the night before.

"Bang on! You're sound. Just what I needed," Moira said. "And I'll grab a couple of those soda breads to take with me."

Well rested and well-fed, Moira said goodbye to her sister and drove the Mini to Glasnevin Cemetery. This was nothing like the quaint and cosy Donnybrook Cemetery she so loved to frequent. With active funerals, visiting loved ones, and scores of curious tourists all vying for place, Moira knew it would be difficult to find a quiet spot to be undisturbed.

The Magdalenes had a memorial near the mass grave where the ashes of the women from the Donnybrook laundry had been reinterred after that property was sold, but there were other Magdalene graves scattered throughout the cemetery. Not being able to identify a specific individual from the markers was no problem, as Moira knew she didn't have to be in close proximity to an individual's gravesite to make contact with them.

She found a bench in a relatively quiet section of very old stones and sat down to wait. Once her thoughts were settled and she felt calm, she opened her mind to the Otherside. Projecting her thoughts into the ether, she sent out a petition of a more general nature than perhaps she should have …

I'm here to speak with the women who fell victim to abuse, neglect, persecution and injustice in the Magdalene Laundries, Mother and Baby Homes, Industrial Schools … On behalf of one of your children, I am seeking Anne Carmody, also known as Cara Moore, or someone who knows of her. I'm here to help.

She had barely finished her petition when a cacophony of voices assaulted her. The sound came from all directions and was like the flapping of thousands of bird wings, the cries of gulls, the rumbling of a train, growing louder and louder. She could make out only a few responses:

Did you find my Billy?

I'm here!

Please help!

I can't rest!

Finally …

Moira fell to her knees, covering her ears with her arms, which she knew was futile, as the voices were in her mind. A sob escaped her lips, and she shuddered, trying to escape the onslaught.

Then a familiar voice broke through: *ENOUGH!*

Give the poor child space. She's trying to help you.

The din slowly subsided until Moira release her arms and raised her head.

"Maimeó! I —" Moira could barely speak and again, choked out a sob.

"You're alright, a leanbh. I wish you'd called on me first and we could have done this together. But it looks like everyone is here now, so you can get on with it."

"Everyone?" Moira inquired.

"The spirits of the Magdalenes — buried here and elsewhere — who have been yearning for help these many years," Nana Brigid explained.

"But I can't help them all! There must be hundreds here!"

"Thousands. It's not all on your shoulders. Others are beginning to reach out and help as well. All will have recompense and redress. There is all eternity ahead to make things right. But I understand you are here on a specific mission."

"Cecilia Carmody — though that's not an accurate surname. Her mother was given the name of Anne Carmody when she entered the laundry. Is she here? We weren't even sure if she was still alive or not," Moira explained.

I'm here. One voice from the waiting crowd.

You are Cecilia's ma?

I am her seanmháthair.

I will let you two visit while I attend to the multitudes …

And Brigid O'Brien left.

CHAPTER 28

—

Maireann croí éadrom i bhfad
A light heart lives longest.

—Irish Proverb

A group of tourists led by a museum guide approached and Moira continued her telepathic conversation with the spirit while sitting sedately on the bench.

You are Cecilia's grandmother?

It was I who began this generational journey through hell. I have been watching over my granddaughter and rejoiced when she reached out to your mother. I knew you three would be effective in ending our family nightmare. I sent Nuala a dream — did she share it with you? A peek into the beginning of the spiral.

I'd like to hear your story from yourself.

My name is Lucy Moore. I was fifteen. Colm was my first boyfriend. I was naïve. He was two years older. I was flattered that he liked me. It was so long ago now, but I remember the headiness of it all. He was gliondar mo chroí. I though he loved me. He may have, but he never got the chance to prove it. One day my da discovered I was pregnant, the next day I found myself in a car with a stranger on my way to St. Gerald's Mother and Baby Home in Dublin. It wasn't so bad there, and I kept my spirits up in the hope that once my baby was born, we would be able to return home together. I just knew once Ma and Da held my little one, their hearts would melt, and we would all be a family together.

I didn't hear from any of my family or Colm for the six months that I was there awaiting Cara's birth. I named her after my seanmháthair, Nana Cara Moore. But I only got to hold her for a moment, and she was swept out of my arms. After that I only saw her across the courtyard in the baby pens, watched over by the nuns. I was allowed to see her for one hour each day. Neither of us went 'home.'

My heart — and my breasts — ached for my darling babby; she now was gliondar mo chroí to me. I wrote to my family asking when I could come home, but I never got a response. The sisters told me I had disgraced them, and they didn't want me back. As soon as I had recovered from childbirth, I was moved to the laundries. There, every day was either scut work or prayers on our knees from seven in the morning to seven at night when we dropped of exhaustion into our cots. I didn't know what happened to Cara for a long time — it could have been years — until one sister, who was more kind than the rest, told me she was sent to St. Cyra's Industrial School for Girls. It seemed no one wanted a bogging bastard child either. This Sister Agnes is the one who told me they renamed my daughter Anne Carmody, so she wouldn't be stained with my name.

I didn't last long after that. My heart was broken as well as my spirit. They had taken everything from me — first my family, my clothes, my name. Then my child, my dignity, my will to live. I heard them say it was a heart attack, but I was only twenty -seven. My heart just stopped. I willed it to stop, I think. It was the only prayer of mine in that place that was ever answered.

Is Anne, or I should say, Cara, here with you now?

She is not. I continue to watch over her at Saint Martha's Nursing Centre. You were so close! Good luck getting past Mother Fachtna — she's a real geebag.

At that moment Nana Brigid appeared and indicated to Lucy that it was time to go. When she disappeared with a slight bow to Moira, Brigid said:

It was my turn to visit with you! You must know how precious you are to me; how proud I am of your efforts on behalf of these Others.

Maimeó, there's something I don't understand.

What is it, child?

Why is it that some, like Riley, accept, forgive, move on, while others are tormented, stuck and unable to move forward from this life?

Ah, a very thoughtful question! I believe I told you once that we take with us to the Otherside our attitudes, character traits and personality. Well, our experiences and circumstances while in the world shape our state of being when we arrive here also. Riley was loved, knew who she was, was well-adjusted. She was grounded in a nurturing support system of family and friends while in the world.

These women in particular were stripped of their identities, torn from anyone who might have loved them. They were treated as less-than-human. That's a lot of hurt and baggage to unpack before they are well enough mentally, spiritually and emotionally to move on. Sometimes the worst thing someone can do to you is not to hurt your body, even to kill the body, but to damage your psyche, your inner being.

Just reaching out to them, letting them see that they are

not forgotten, that someone recognises them as having value and are worthy of kindness and love, goes a long way towards healing. You and your sisters are doing a great work here, one soul at a time. Don't ever doubt it.

Chapter 29

Ní bhíonn in aon rud ach seal.
Nothing lasts forever.

—Irish Proverb

"It's back to Saint Martha's Nursing Centre, then," Deirdre said after Moira returned and reported her experience to her sister.

"Do we ask to see Anne Carmody or Cara Moore?" Moira wondered out loud.

"I believe our best chance is to not ask for her by name, but to take Cecilia with us and ask to see her mother," Deirdre said.

"Sound idea," Moira agreed.

Cecelia was gobsmacked that they had discovered who

and where her mother was located. She and Eamon were heading home from Schull the next morning and would take a detour through Dublin on their way to Roscommon. After consulting with Nuala, the sisters had arranged for the couple to stop at Hawthorn House in Kildare for the night, then Nuala would join them for the rest of the journey to Dublin the following day.

"Do we call ahead and make an appointment?" Moira asked of Deirdre.

"I wouldn't put it past Sister Fachtna to spirit Anne away before we could arrive if she knew we were coming. Let's get word to Sister Bernadette and enlist her help once again."

It was difficult for the two sisters to wait and not rush over to the nursing home and confront Mother Superior, but after giving Sister Bernadette the information they had regarding Anne Carmody/Cara Moore, she assured them that Anne was a resident and she, herself would be there to facilitate their visit.

The party met outside the nursing home at the agreed upon time of eleven o'clock the next morning. Nuala made the introductions for this first in-person meeting. Cecilia was a bundle of nerves; Eamon held her hand and tried to comfort her.

"No matter what happens, we're okay. You're okay.

We have a grand family. We'll get through this together."

They rang the bell, and Sister Bernadette opened it and beckoned them in with a finger to her lips.

"I didn't even tell Sister Fachtna you were coming. Visiting hours just started and I've put Anne is a quiet corner of the lounge."

"Did you tell her who I was?" Cecilia asked.

"I thought it best to leave that up to you, what you wanted to tell her. She is a verra quiet person, doesn't say much these many years here."

"How long has she been here?" Deirdre asked.

"Let's see … I've been here since we began taking in the Magdalenes from the laundry side in 1992. She was in the first group that arrived. They moved me here from the convent in Dublin. I can't say how long she was at the laundry. Here we are," Bernadette said as she pushed open a set of double doors that led to a spacious meeting room with rows of tables and chairs. "Anne is the one sitting in that rocking chair in the corner. She likes to rock …"

Anne was in an alcove of the lounge where there was a couch and some chairs away from the main part of the room. Bernadette laid her hand on the woman's shoulder, and she started with a cry of "oh!"

"It's alright dear, you've got some visitors," Bernadette said.

"Visitors?"

"This is Cecilia and her friends, come to chat."

Anne looked up through cataract-clouded eyes, squinting slightly. "Hello?"

Cecilia pulled up a chair in front of the rocker and sat. Eamon, Deirdre, Moira and Nuala took the couch opposite.

"Hello, my name is Cecilia Carmody. Does that name mean anything to you?"

"I don't think so ... should it?"

Cecilia looked back at Eamon, who just shrugged. Deirdre gave her an encouraging nod.

Cecilia continued, "I was born in St. Gerald's Mother and Baby Home in Dublin in 1955. My mother was Anne Carmody."

"That's my name too," Anne said. Her head bowed, chin resting on her chest.

"It is. My mother was also known as Cara Moore."

At that, Anne raised her head and looked intently at Cecilia. "Who are you?"

"I believe I am your daughter."

Anne gave a little cry, her hands going to her mouth. Sister Bernadette went to her side, crouched down and put an arm around the woman.

"Are you alright, dear? Your daughter has been

searching for you for many years and has finally found you."

"My daughter …" She reached out her hands. "Come closer, my eyes don't work so good anymore."

Cecilia stood and knelt in front of her mother. She took her two hands in her own. "I'm here, Ma. I'm so sorry it took me so long to find you."

"And have you had a good life, dear?"

"I've got a wonderful husband. That's him there — his name is Eamon. We have three beautiful children. Your grandchildren."

"My grandchildren …"

"And you, Ma? Can you tell me about your life?"

Just then they were interrupted by Mother Fachtna coming into the room.

"What is all this? What are you doing here?"

"Cecilia's visiting her mother. It is within visiting hours, so I thought it would be alright. They've signed in the guest book as required …" Sister Bernadette said.

"That will be all, Sister. You may report to the kitchens to help with lunch," the Mother Superior said dismissively.

Sister Bernadette bowed to Mother Fachtna, turned and bowed to the group on the couch and then to Cecilia and quietly left the room.

"Who told you this was your mother?"

At that, Moira stood up. "I did."

"And how did you come by this information?"

"I am not at liberty to reveal my sources, but I know that Anne's original name was Cara Moore. Her mother was Lucy Moore, who spent gruelling, humiliating years in one of your laundries and died there of a broken heart after her daughter, Anne here, was torn from her. I know Anne or Cara, has been a virtual prisoner of Catholic institutions all her life."

"You think you know quite a bit about things you actually know nothing about. We care for these women. We give them homes when their families disown them or can't care for them. We teach them and put a roof over their heads and food in their mouths. Who are you to call them prisoners?"

"Is my mother free to leave here?" Cecilia interjected.

"Well —"

"If not, then she is a prisoner. Her life has been stolen from her. Eamon and I had vowed that if and when we found her, we would care for her. She is coming home with me, and that will be the end of your government payments for at least one of your victims."

"This is the only home this woman has known for the past twenty years. Why don't you ask her if she wants to leave," Mother Fachtna challenged.

Cecelia turned back to her mother, knelt once again in front of her and took her hands in her own.

"Mother, I've come to take you home. Are you willing to come with me?"

"You mean I can leave here? I have paid my penance and am finally free to go?"

"You are."

This time Anne's hands flew to cover her whole face, and she began to shake with sobs.

"Is that a good enough answer for you?" Deirdre asked Mother Fachtna.

"I will draw up the paperwork." The nun then turned on her heels and left the room.

Chapter 30

I ndiaidh a chéile a thógtar na caisleáin.
Rome was not built in a day.

—Irish Proverb

Sister Bernadette arrived and announced she had been assigned to walk them back to Anne's room and help her gather her things. The Gallaghers and Eamon agreed they would wait in the car. Cecilia took Anne's arm, and they followed the nun down a hallway and entered a small room about two and a half by three and a half metres. In it was a single bed, a nightstand with a table lamp, a wardrobe and chest of drawers. Sister Bernadette had brought with her a cardboard box and Cecilia began to help Anne deposit her belongings into the box: one dress ("for Mass"), two pairs of trousers, three blouses ("I sometimes spill and have to change"), three changes of undergarments.

Cecilia opened the drawer in the bedside table. In it was a Bible and a set of rosary beads.

"Will you be taking these?" Cecilia asked Anne.

Anne glanced over and said, "I'll take the Bible. I gave up on the rosary some time ago. Reciting the rosary seemed more of a punishment than a prayer."

With Cecilia carrying her box, Anne walked resolutely out the door of the little chamber she had lived in for the past twenty years without a backward glance. They stopped in Mother Superior's office where the head nun had a piece of paper on the desk for Anne to sign.

"I would like to read it first," Cecilia said.

"Would you read it to me, please?" Anne said.

"It's just a standard release statement," Mother Fachtna said.

Cecilia began to read:

"I, Anne Carmody, am voluntarily leaving the care of Saint Martha's Nursing Centre and agree to not hold liable the Sisters of Our Lady of Hope or the staff of the nursing centre for any past —" Cecilia stopped reading. She turned to Anne and said, "Do you have any problem with me crossing out everything after the first 'Centre' here?"

"Not at all, dear."

Cecilia left only 'I, Anne Carmody, am voluntarily leaving the care of Saint Martha's Nursing Centre,' blacked out the rest with the pen then offered the instrument to Anne to sign. Her hands shook, but the signature was legible: *Anne Carmody, or Cara Moore.*

Then without another word to the nun behind the desk, the two walked out.

The Gallaghers and Eamon were waiting by the cars as they crossed the car park.

"I still don't understand how you found me," Anne said.

"It was the Gallaghers here who found you. I hired them to help me. It didn't take long at all before they knew where you were."

"That's wonderful. Wonderful. I thought I was invisible."

"Maybe one day we will tell you the story of our search," Moira said with a smile.

"I would like to treat all you lovely lasses to lunch!" Eamon said. "Who's up for some bangers and mash, or a short rib of beef?"

"Meat? I don't remember ever having meat …" Anne said.

"I think we need to let your little family get acquainted. Nuala can come with us, and we'll get her back to Kildare. We'll be in touch — we'd love to know how you are getting along," Deirdre said.

"Thank you for all you've done for us," Cecilia said. "I will call you later."

On the drive to Kildare to return Nuala to Hawthorn House, Moira told the tale of her Glasnevin visit.

"Thousands?" Nuala exclaimed.

"That's what Nana Brigid said."

"Those poor women! What can we do for so many?"

"I've been thinking … we could join the JFM group — if they'll have us, not being victims or related to victims — and lend our assistance through them," Deirdre said.

"That's cracking, Deirdre! We may not be able to help them all, but one-by-one we can do something for some," Moira said.

Chapter 31

Aithníonn ciaróg ciaróg eile
It takes one to know one.

—Irish Proverb

Two weeks later Cecilia called.

"Eamon has taken Ma out for breakfast, so I thought I'd call and give you an update of how she's adjusting. Do you have a minute or two?"

"Absolutely! We haven't stopped thinking about Cara. How are things going?" Deirdre inquired.

"She's like a little child! Everything is new — do you know, she's never had a cup of coffee? Nor anything sweet — no biscuits, no sugar on her oats, never a birthday cake. Well, maybe the no sugar isn't such a bad thing, but such complete deprivation!"

"Has she opened up at all about her past, how she got to the industrial school?"

"Bit by bit. Each time we talk, there's a reluctance at first, but with encouragement, she starts talking and then it's like the floodgates open up. I think it's therapeutic for her to get it out.

"She remembers being about four years old and starting school. She was scared to leave the Home but doesn't remember her ma at all. Even at that age they had chores to do. She remembers scrubbing the steps with a little brush and a bucket. It was fun at first, a child doing grownup work, but not so much after years of the same.

"It was drilled into her, and others like her, that they were children of sin, in need of constant penance and repentance. Seems the school motto was through the power of prayer, cleanliness and abstaining from the pleasures of the flesh — which evidently included sufficient food and sleep — and working beyond all human endurance, they would be saved. With daily Mass and weekly confession, she came to know and like the young priest who was assigned to the school. A coveted job among the girls was bringing the priest his nightly glass of milk and digestive biscuit. He was kind and treated her as a human being.

"As she told the tale, I got this sinking feeling — a foreboding of not good things to come. And I was right. He was grooming her. When she was about fourteen (she's not sure of her age, as they didn't celebrate birthdays), on one of her assigned days to bring his evening snack, he produced a second glass and offered to share the milk with her. She drank it but remembers nothing after. I believe she was drugged and then raped.

"The next day she was 'sick' and stayed in bed. She was 'sore down there and bleeding,' were her words. Fifty odd years later, she still couldn't describe what happened."

"That's abominable! Her story has to be told to someone who can do something about this. Do you know if this priest is still an active minister?" Moira asked.

"As of yet, she hasn't even said his name, so I don't know. After the incident of the shared milk, she was never assigned to that chore again. Of course, it wasn't long before her pregnancy began to show. She had no idea what was happening to her or her body. The nuns said she must be carrying the devil's child and made no inquiries into how it could have happened under their vigilant watch. I can tell you this much —Ma did *not* have a boyfriend!

"Well, the same thing happened to her that happened to her ma. She was sent to the Mother and Baby Home until I was born, then I went into foster care, and she went into the laundries. And she thought she was worked hard in the Industrial School!

"Now it wasn't just original sin, or the sins of the mother for which she had to atone, she was a fallen woman, dirty and wicked. Jaysus, Mary, and Joseph it's a miracle she isn't addled in the brain! I think I would have taken my own life in a place like that, or at least tried."

"Have you gotten any counselling for her?" Deirdre asked.

"As yet, she hasn't talked to any of the counsellors the JFM have on staff for victims, but I'm hoping she'll give it a lash."

"Have you introduced her to your children?" Moira wanted to know.

"Oh, that is therapy indeed! My youngest daughter, Rose, brought her family over a few days ago. They live in Tralee and stayed with us for a few days. She has three weans all under ten years of age. Ma lit up like a Christmas tree to see those little ones. She fussed over them and got down on the floor playing their games with them. The oldest, Róisín, read to Ma from her Bible. She says she doesn't see well, but I believe she also never really learned to read well. Wasn't much of a school of learning as far as I can tell.

"Oh! Gotta go! I hear the car returning. Thank you again for rescuing her from those gowls."

"I only wish we could have gotten to her sooner. To think she was just a few miles away from you all these years!" Moira said.

"You will be forever in our prayers," Cecilia replied.

GONE BUT NOT FORGOTTEN

CHAPTER 32

—

Is ait an mac an saol
Life is strange.

—Irish Proverb

January 6, 2013

To: Moira, Deirdre, Nuala

From: Katie

Subject: Your expertise

Greetings cousins! We went back home to New England for Christmas and Ma introduced us to her friend, a first-generation immigrant from the Old Country. She told a tale of grief and loss that I believe warrants your attention. Let me know if your schedule allows you to take on a (paying!) client in the near future. If so, I'll send details and put you in touch with Mrs. O'Reilly.

Cheers!

January 8, 2013

To: Katie

From: Deirdre

Cc Nuala, Moira

Re: Your expertise

Athbhliain faoi mhaise dhuit! Happy New Year! Thanks for getting in touch. We are willing and ready to help out your ma's friend. Send details.

Any plans for another vacation in the Emerald Isle? Slán,

Deirdre & Co.

January 12, 2013

To Moira, Deirdre, Nuala

From: Katie

Cc: Mary O'Reilly

Re: Your expertise

Thanks!

Her name is Mary O'Reilly (I've cc'd her here — she

doesn't like to use email, but says she'll give it a lash!) Her parents, Aoibh and Shay Collins, emigrated to Canada in 1956 along with their 8 children. The thing is, Mary's mum had NINE children, but they left the youngest, Niamh, behind in Cork with a neighbor. I know! Can you believe it? Their oldest was 18 and a son who could help his dad. Mary, at age 5, was closest to her baby sister. The children were told it was only temporary and the neighbors — Imogen and Declan Sullivan — were planning to emigrate as well within the year and join them in Ontario. They were childless and had taken a shine to the golden-haired little girl. They doted on her, something she couldn't get from the harried mother of 9.

For the first few months the Sullivans wrote often, sending photographs of Niamh. The Collinses sent cards and little gifts and looked forward to being reunited. But soon after Niamh's fourth birthday, they never heard from the Sullivans again. They didn't emigrate to Canada or anywhere else, as far as Mary's family knows, and dropped all contact with them.

Mary's parents and siblings are all deceased now except her older brother, John, who is 64 this year. Neither can forget their little sister and are yearning to know what happened to her.

If you can make any inroads into this mystery, the

siblings are pooling their resources to finance your search.

I've copied Mary here and will let you continue this discussion with her.

Thank you! Thank you! And yes, Alex and I would love a second trip to Ireland this summer once school is out. Maybe combine it with a ferry jaunt to England? We'll let you know our plans as they unfold. Bye for now, Katie

CHAPTER 33

Giorraíonn beirt bóthar
Two shorten the road.

—Irish Proverb

"Alright, ladies, any ideas for helping Mary and John find their sister?" Deirdre said, as she and Moira joined Nuala on a group call.

"Well, if Niamh is still alive, she's in her sixties now, and most likely doesn't go by her maiden name or Sullivan. I can check for marriage records to find her. What was her surname before being left with the Sullivans?" Nuala asked.

"Mary has sent us a listing of all the family information. Let's see … I've got it here … The last name is Collins," Deirdre replied.

"Nuala, maybe you can follow up on the Sullivans as well. Check to see if they are on any emigration lists. Just because they didn't let the Collinses know, doesn't mean they didn't leave Ireland," Moira suggested. "I'll check for deaths. Maybe they all died and that's why they didn't communicate."

"Death won't stop the communication now, with Moira on the case!" Nuala laughed.

"Land records will tell us if they sold their place in Cork. I've got the last known address here from Mary as well. I'll look into that," Deirdre offered.

"Looks like we've got our assignments. Let's check back in a few days and see what we've come up with," Moira said.

Once they disconnected from Nuala, Deirdre said, "How about a road trip? We could visit Ma and stop in Cork on the way south. I'd like to find this address, maybe talk to neighbours. Fifty-seven years isn't *that* long ago. Maybe someone remembers them."

"That's sound. I can be ready to go day after tomorrow," Moira replied.

Two days later the sisters had packed the Mini Cooper to include Suki, their Anatolian Shepherd. They usually didn't take her on their research trips, preferring to leave her in the care of their dog-sitter, Billy, but a trip to Schull without her would not go down well with Ma, who adored the dog. For Suki, the feeling was mutual.

The close to six-hour drive all the way to Schull was a bit long for Suki so they arranged to stay overnight in Youghal with their O'Brien cousins. From there they could check out the last known address of the Sullivan family in nearby Midleton.

Taking the scenic coastal route from Dublin, their first stop was in Greystone, to let Suki run along the beach and stretch her long legs. Not being of a water-loving species, she preferred to chase the gulls that ventured onto the beach. After a half hour she was ready for a nap, and they continued on to Youghal with the dog asleep most of the time.

Shannon, wife of their cousin, Darren O'Brien, greeted them at the door as they pulled up to the one-story brick detached home in an estate just off the N25.

"Welcome! How you getting on? It's been too long!" Shannon exclaimed, giving her cousins hugs and making an immediate new friend in Suki as she offered a dog treat. "With both kids off to uni now, we've got two spare bedrooms for you. You sure you can only stay the one night?"

"We appreciate your hospitality, but we do need to get down to Schull to see Ma. We might stop again on the return if you don't mind, though," Deirdre said.

"Absolutely! Darren will be home in a couple hours, and we'll have some good craic reminiscing. Is it possible we haven't seen you since your da's funeral?"

"I think that's right. You saw Nuala when you were kind enough to host her during her culinary schooling, but it's been donkey's years since Moira and I have been here."

"Ah, Nuala! What a wonderful time we had with her here going through her course. She would practice every day, and we were the beneficiaries of her newly acquired culinary skills.

"Well, come in and get settled. I want to hear all about this new business of yours Dymphna has told me about. Gallagher Investigations, is it?"

"That's right. I didn't know Ma has been talking about it," Moira said.

"Oh, she's verra proud of you. Says you're helping all sorts of people."

"That's one way of putting it," Deirdre laughed.

After depositing their travel bags in their respective rooms, the sisters rejoined their hostess in the spacious eating area of the kitchen/dining room. They could see through the double French doors into the fenced-in garden where Suki was making the acquaintance of the O'Brien's Irish setter.

"Now what exactly do you do? Dymphna says it has

to do with family history. Are you operating a genealogical research business?" Shannon asked.

"Nuala does most of that part of it for us. She has worked with Ma for several years now and has a sound grasp on that aspect. Deirdre and I ... we consult with clients on various problems such as missing persons, wrongful deaths ... that sort of thing." Deirdre waved her hand in the air in a vague attempt to indicate the many sorts of things they did.

"I see ... I think ..." Shannon said.

"Sure look, would you mind if in the morning we left Suki here for a bit while we check out an address for a client? We can take her, but I think she's enjoying not being in the Mini," Deirdre said, moving off the topic of their business ventures.

"Ah, that would be grand. This is the most fun our Hazel has had since the cat died. The two of them are having a quality time. And I'll be sure to send you off with a big breakfast in the morning."

Chapter 34

Tús maith leath na hoibre.
A good start is half the work.

—Irish Proverb

The next morning, after the promised filling breakfast, they said goodbye to the O'Briens and Suki, and found the address about two kilometres west of the town of Midleton, thirty minutes out from Cork City. It was on the outskirts of the settlement, in a grouping of three homes with scattered farmhouses nearby. The sisters guessed the stone cottage situated on a quarter-acre dated from the 1850s. The place looked abandoned. Tall grass grew wild all around the plot, one window was broken and the whole place had a desolate, forlorn air. Moira and Deirdre walked around the house but observed no signs of life.

"Let's check in with the houses on either side;

hopefully someone is home there," Deirdre said.

They left the Mini Cooper in front of the Sullivan place and walked next door — another stone cottage, but not quite so old, and definitely better taken care of. A young man answered their knock.

"Who is it dear?" A woman's voice called from the recesses.

"Don't know yet," he called over his shoulder. "What's the story?" he directed to the sisters.

"We're trying to find the family who lived next door there," Deirdre said, pointing to the Sullivan cottage.

"No idea. It was like that — falling apart — when we bought this place two years ago. We answered the advert for that one, but it was too banjaxed for us. While we were there the farmer who owned this place approached us and said he'd give us a good deal on his own place if we didn't go through an estate agent. We scooped it up — exactly what we were looking for. Sorry I can't tell you anything about the owners next door."

"Thanks for speaking with us, Slán agat," Deirdre said.

"Slán leat," he replied and closed the door.

They walked to the house on the other side of the Sullivan's and found an ancient-looking woman with gnarled hands grasping a cane standing on the porch.

"Bail ó Dhia ort," she greeted.

"Good day to you! We are looking for the family who used to live next door — the Sullivans?" Deirdre asked.

"Ach! Long gone! The daughter tried to sell it when they passed about twenty years ago now, but no takers. It's been empty that long."

"The daughter … Niamh?" Moira asked.

"That's right. She came by a while ago to check on the place, stopped in to say hello, but I haven't seen her lately."

"She doesn't live in the area?" Deirdre asked.

"She's got a place on the water, Ballycotton, I think," the woman said.

"Do you know the address, or know how we can reach her?" Moira asked.

"You lasses come inside, I had it on a slip of paper once, but it may take me a bit to find it …" she spoke as she turned into the house and Moira and Deirdre followed her inside.

"What did you say your names were?"

"I'm Deirdre Gallagher, and this is my sister, Moira," Deirdre said.

"Gallagher … Gallagher … I used to know some Gallaghers — Sheila and Cian! You related to them?" she asked.

"I don't think so. The names aren't familiar. We are originally from the Skibbereen area, further south," Deirdre said. "And what is your name?"

"Pardon my manners! I'm Riona. Have a seat while I look for that paper … Have a cuppa? I've put the pot on," Riona said.

"None for me, thanks. We don't want to trouble you," Moira said.

"Ah! 'Tis no trouble at all! I was just about to have a cuppa and would love to have you join me."

Moira looked at Deirdre, who nodded slightly. "Alright, then. If you're sure it's not a bother."

"Have you lived here long?" Deirdre asked.

"Came in 1983, just after my Tommy passed. No sense in me rattling around in that big ol' house alone. I knew Imogen Sullivan from bridge club. When I told her I was looking to sell and move to something smaller, she told me about this place. Been here ever since."

"You don't know who lived in this house back in the fifties, do you?" Deirdre asked.

"The fifties? Sure look, wasn't that well before my time!"

"You knew Mrs Sullivan well, then?" Moira asked.

"As well as anyone around here, I'd say. Neither of them had the gift of the gab, but we traded stories and cups of sugar," Riona said.

"Did she ever mention a family named Collins?" Moira questioned.

"Collins? Not that I can remember … but my memory isn't so good anymore."

They sipped their tea and ate a biscuit, then made ready to leave.

"Thank you for the tea and for all the information, Riona," Deirdre said, setting down her teacup. "Can we help with the washing up?"

"I've got it, don't you worry about it. It's been a pleasure having the company. I'm sorry I couldn't find that paper Niamh gave me with her address and phone number. I'd lose my head if it wasn't attached!"

"You've been very helpful. We'll manage. Oh! One more thing. Do you know where the Sullivans are buried?" Moira asked.

"Sure, and they're resting in the graveyard at Holy Rosary Church in Midleton. I can't tell you exactly where, it was lashing down the day they buried both of them, and my arthritis was bad …"

"They both died the same day? Was it an accident?" Deirdre asked.

"Pneumonia. It was about this time of year, too. Damp and cold seeps into your bones. Declan come down with it first, then Imogen got it from him, nursing him like she did. Died within days of one another."

Chapter 35

Ná scald do liopaí le leite fear eile
Never scald your lips with another man's porridge.

—Irish Proverb

"Where to now?" Deirdre asked Moira after returning to the Mini Cooper. "We can't go knocking on every door in Ballycotton," Deirdre said.

"Can't we?" Moira replied.

Just then Deirdre's mobile rang: Nuala.

"Hey, Sis! What's the craic?"

"I've got death dates for the Sullivans. They died within days of each other in January of 1995 — the twentieth and twenty-second," Nuala said.

"Thanks, Nuala, but what we really need is the location of their graves in the Holy Rosary Church in Midleton," Deirdre replied.

"What? How do you know that? I've just barely accessed their burial information on the Irish Graveyards website."

"We found a talkative neighbour, but she didn't know the exact location and we don't have the time to wander around the place reading every marker."

"Right. They are in plot number 420 section B. That should get you to the spot. There might even be a map and index on site if you're lucky."

"Any luck with Niamh's current surname?" Deirdre asked.

"I couldn't find any record of a marriage for her, and so far, nothing has come up for an address or phone either. But I'll keep looking."

"I guess we'll head to the cemetery then, see if that leads anywhere. Thanks a million, Nuala! Slán!"

"Tabhair aire," Nuala replied.

"I have an idea," Moira said, pulling out her notebook and tearing out a sheet. "Let's pick up some polybags in Midleton before we go to the cemetery. We can write a note and leave it on the Sullivan graves. January twentieth is in a couple days. If she's still living nearby, maybe she'll visit the graves on the anniversary of their deaths and find our note."

"That's cracking, Moira! And maybe you'll have an encounter when we're there ..."

"I've felt nothing from anyone yet, not even wandering around their old cottage. But we can certainly give it a lash," Moira replied.

While Moira drove, Deirdre composed the note.

"How's this: Searching for Niamh Sullivan, born Collins, whose family emigrated to Canada in 1956. Her brother and sister are anxious to find her. We are representing her sister, Mary Collins O'Reilly, and would like to speak with you if you are this person. Please ring this number: 01 555 3113. Deirdre Gallagher."

"Perfect. Now let's find a place to get copies made so we can also post it on the door of every house in Ballycotton!"

They found a Tesco in Midleton and purchased the polybags and a roll of Sellotape. Finding the grave site was not quite so easy, as the hoped-for map and index for the cemetery was not to be found. The sections were marked though, and they located Section B without too much difficulty. They parked the Mini and put a call through to Nuala.

"There's no map. Can you pull one up on your computer and give us an idea where plot 420 is located?" Deirdre asked when Nuala picked up.

"Give me a sec —" Nuala replied. Then after a moment, "Here it is! If you're standing with your back to the church facing the graveyard, it's the far-right row, the very end."

"Bang on! Thanks again, Nuala. You've saved us hours of stone-reading!"

"Cheers!"

Deirdre walked ahead and found the Sullivan plot. She read the inscription aloud, "'Declan Brian Sullivan born 1916, died 20 January 1995. Imogen Mary, his wife born 1917, died 22 January 1995. Gone but not forgotten.' Look, Moira, fresh flowers on the graves! Maybe Niamh came early for the anniversary," Deirdre speculated.

"That would be unfortunate. Well, let's leave the note anyway, and now all the more reason to canvas Ballycotton. At least Riona said her place was on the sea, so maybe if we start targeting the houses along the coastal road first, we'll get lucky," Moira suggested.

"Do you want to stay here a while and see if you can make contact with either of the Sullivans?" Deirdre asked.

"It wouldn't hurt. It's begun spitting a bit, but that just lends itself to the mood. You can sit in the car and wait if you'd like," Moira said.

"I'm grand. I'm going to walk among the stones. I'll check back with you later."

There were benches placed throughout the cemetery and Moira selected one not too far away from the Sullivan plot. She closed her eyes and breathed deeply. She focused her thoughts on that tiny girl so many years ago who most likely had no idea she would never see her ma and da again. How many memories do we retain from that early age? Would she even remember that she once had a different family? Does she remember the older sister who doted on her and the brothers who must have teased her and carried her about?

The wind picked up and Moira saw Deirdre pull her anorak tighter around her and begin to head back to the car. Then in the wind, Moira heard a wail, followed by the words, *I know we did wrong. I tried to tell her it wasn't right, but she wouldn't give her up.*

The form of a tall, thin man appeared before her. His head was bowed, and he wrung his hands in a repetitive motion.

Declan? Is Imogen with you?

She wouldn't come. She's always been stubborn. She refuses to acknowledge her wrongdoing. Of course I loved that little one, and I continued to love the young woman she became. But it wasn't right. She wasn't ours to keep. I can't do anything to make it right now.

We can help. There is always a way. Feeling badly about it is the first step.

She comes every Sunday and brings us flowers. I tried over and over to tell her I'm sorry, but she can't hear me. But you can hear me! Will you tell her for me? It's something I should have said while I was alive, but I'm saying it now ...

Declan, don't go yet! Moira said as he began to fade. *Can you tell me where Niamh lives?*

Carnation Cottage ... And he was gone.

Chapter 36

Múineann gá seift.
Necessity is the mother of invention.

—Irish Proverb

The rain was lashing down now as Moira ran to the Mini Cooper.

"Tears from heaven?" Deirdre asked as Moira shook off her anorak and climbed in.

"Tears of remorse, it seems," she replied. "Declan is repentant of keeping the child, Niamh, but Imogen refused to even see me. He asked me to tell Niamh he's sorry."

"Did he also tell you how to find her to deliver this message?"

"All he said was 'Carnation Cottage.' I'm assuming that's in Ballycotton, so it's a starting place. Ready to head that way?"

"Let's call Shannon first and check to see if it's okay

to keep Suki there longer. We've been gone several hours now as it is." Deirdre was Suki's person, and the dog was never far from her mind, if not from her side.

"Do it," Moira agreed.

Deirdre made the call and Shannon reported that she and Darren were at the park with both Suki and Hazel, and from all appearances, the craic was ninety.

"Take your time. We'll be here whenever you arrive."

"Thanks a million, Shannon! We're headed to Ballycotton, so we'll check in again soon."

There was no An Post in Ballycotton proper, so the sisters stopped at the garda station for directions.

"Carnation House? You'll be looking for the artist, Niamh Sullivan, then?" the guard on the desk asked.

"That we are!" Deirdre replied.

"You're fans then; she's quite popular with the tourists and locals alike."

He pulled out a leaflet of the town with a small map on the inside. Putting an X on a spot along the coastal road, he said, "You'll find her here, if she's not out along the beach painting rocks and waves and such."

Taking the map, they drove the short distance and

found the tiny cottage that couldn't have been more than 500 square feet. The roof was thatch and Deirdre guessed it must have been built before the last century. No one answered their knock, so they attached the note to the door, left their car parked out front and walked down to the shore. It had turned into a soft day, with just a light mist, but still not the type of day one would want to be out painting in.

"An artist, and a popular one at that! Maybe she is at one of the art galleries we passed coming into the village," Deirdre suggested.

"Or she may be out getting the messages. She could be anywhere! Do we just sit parked outside her door and wait?" Moira asked.

"I don't know about you but I'm starving. Let's grab something to eat while we're waiting," Deirdre said.

They found a pub called The Raven and ordered fish and chips. While they ate, Deirdre noticed a row of lovely watercolour paintings lining the walls. She went over to get a closer look and saw they were signed *NSully*.

The seascapes were moody and muted, full of atmosphere. There was one of the Ballycotton lighthouse that was especially moving. They all had price stickers on them.

"That's a class one — my favourite, actually, but I'm

willing to let it go to an appreciative buyer." The bartender stood beside her, indicating the lighthouse painting.

"I'm interested in the artist, Niamh Sullivan?"

"That's right. She has her larger ones in The Gallery in the village, but I take in a few to show and sell for her. I'm Jacob Branagán, the owner of The Raven." He held out his hand to her.

"Deirdre Gallagher. My sister and I are trying to find Ms Sullivan. Know where she might be?"

"She's got a show going on at The Gallery this week; might find her there."

"Thanks! And my compliments to your chef — the chips are spot on!"

"That would be me as well, so I thank you!"

Deirdre returned to their table and filled Moira in on what she'd learned.

They finished their meal and left a generous tip. They found The Gallery, which had a handful of lookers moving between the paintings. They were approached by a woman dressed in herringbone trousers and matching blazer, crisp white blouse underneath.

"Welcome to The Gallery, I'm Shauna, can I interest you in anything in particular? We are highlighting three local artists this week."

"We'd like to just look around for a few minutes, if

that's okay," Deirdre said.

"Of course! Take your time. I'll be wandering around if you have any questions. And feel free to help yourself to a beverage and hors d'oeuvres." She wandered away to speak with a couple standing in front of a giant abstract that might have been an ocean scene.

The room was sectioned off by moveable partitions so that each of the three featured artists had their works in their own niche section of the gallery. One was a male, another a young woman in her twenties, and the third had to be Niamh. Her hair was grey, cut short in a bob. She wore a soft grey wool midi dress belted at the waist that perfectly accentuated her trim figure.

Now that they'd found her, the sisters were somewhat at a loss as to how to approach her, as they hadn't practiced a speech. As usual in these situations, Moira deferred to her older, if only by ten months, and more worldly-wise sister.

"Ms Sullivan?" Deirdre began, walking up to her with her hand outstretched.

The woman took the proffered hand and replied, "Thank you for coming in today."

"My name is Deirdre Gallagher, and this is my sister, Moira. We saw your paintings in The Raven just now. You do beautiful work."

"Thank you," she repeated.

"We are not here to discuss your art, though. We were hoping to be able to speak to you in private. Is there a place we can meet after you are finished here?"

"An unusual request. What is this about?"

"It's a family matter. We have been hired by your family to find you."

"My family? I have no family. You must have the wrong person."

"You are Niamh Sullivan, born to Aoibh and Shay Collins, who emigrated to Canada when you were three years old?"

The colour drained from Niamh's face, and she shakily sat down on a nearby chair.

"Who did you say you were?"

We are Moira and Deirdre Gallagher, of Gallagher Investigations. Your sister, Mary, and brother, John, have hired us to find you."

"I think you're right. We need to go somewhere private to discuss this," Niamh said as a couple with two children in tow entered the space. "The Gallery is open until half-five. That's an hour from now. I'll meet you back at The Raven then."

"Slán go fóill," Deirdre said.

"Slán go fóill."

Chapter 37

*Ag tuileadh agus ag trá a chaitheann an
fharraige an lá.*
The tide spends the day going in and out.
—Irish Proverb

"Can't get enough of our chips, eh?" Jacob called out as the sisters returned to The Raven. "Did you find Niamh?"

"We did; we've arranged to meet with her here."

"Bang on! I'll seat you in a corner where you can more easily chat."

"That would be grand, thanks a million," Deirdre said.

They ordered drinks and talked about what they should say to Niamh.

"You know I prefer to be upfront with people about my sources of information, but I believe the more important issue here is that her family is and has been searching for her, regardless of how we went about accomplishing that," Moira began.

"I agree. I hope she comes …"

"You think she might not?" Moira asked, surprised.

"She may think we are scammers or something. There's a lot of sketchy people out there acting the maggot," Deirdre said.

Just then Niamh appeared at their table.

"I left early. Shauna is watching my section. Now what is this about?" Niamh said as she slipped into the booth.

"Our American cousin, Katie, is a neighbour to your sister, Mary Collins O'Reilly. Mary and your brother, John, have been looking for you for a very long time. When they heard from Katie about our agency here in Ireland, which specialises in investigations of this kind, they got in touch and hired us to find you."

"Mary is married … to an O'Reilly …" Niamh said.

Deirdre glanced at Moira, who shrugged.

"Are you alright, Ms Sullivan?" Deirdre asked.

"Niamh. Call me Niamh. I don't know. This is all so much to take in. They haven't forgotten about me?"

"Of course not! I don't know how much the Sullivans told you — you were so young at the time. Your separation from your family was supposed to be temporary. The Sullivans were so attached to you, they couldn't bear to have you leave them. But they were also planning to emigrate to Canada soon after your family left. I don't know when they changed their minds, or if they ever really intended to leave, but they stopped correspondence with your family and that was it. They basically kept you for their own."

"They said they loved me — all the time. But the older I got, the more I felt smothered by that love. I guess they must have been so afraid of losing me that they were very strict. I wasn't allowed to go anywhere if they weren't with me. As you can imagine, that didn't lend itself to much of a social life."

"Do you remember the Collinses? Were you too young to remember you had another family?"

"I remember Mary. I forgot her name until you said it just now, but I remember her playing with me. I think I remember Mother. It was a noisy place with lots of kids running around. I liked going to the Sullivans because they had lots of sweets, and it was quiet. After a while I asked where my ma was, and I was told that they were my ma and da now. Mrs Sullivan said my family had too many children and they didn't want me anymore."

"Jeanie Mac! That's brutal!" Deirdre exclaimed.

"I've been in counselling for some time now, and my therapist says that's why I haven't been able to have a long-term relationship with anyone. I don't feel loveable or wanted, despite the protestations to the contrary that the Sullivans loved me.

"But tell me about Mary and … John, you say? Which one was he? How old are they both now?"

Moira pulled the pedigree chart from her bag that Mary had sent and set it in front of Niamh.

"These are your parents' names, and this is the list of all their children. You see Mary was born right before you, so she is sixty-two now, and John before her, is sixty-four."

"And all these others? They are all gone?"

"Mary and John are the only living children besides yourself," Deirdre said.

"I never knew them … just names on a piece of paper. How is that fair?"

"Well, it certainly isn't love," Moira said, and Deirdre gave her a sharp look.

"When can I see them? Are they coming here?" Niamh said, the eagerness evident in her voice.

"That is a bit problematic," Deirdre said. "John has Parkinson's Disease, and although he's still healthy in many ways, he has acute anxiety as his main symptom and Mary says there is no way she can get him on an airplane. Mary said she would come as soon as we found you, but another option is that they are willing to pay for you to fly to America."

"Do you know why I bought this place in Ballycotton? Well, besides it being an art community … I wanted to be near the ocean. I imagined in my childish brain that my family sailed away from me across the ocean. I keep watching for them to return the same way …"

By now, tears were flowing down Niamh's cheeks and Deirdre too, brushed back a tear.

"How did you find me?" Niamh asked.

And there it is, thought Moira.

"It's just what we do," said Deirdre. "Our sister, Nuala, is brilliant with genealogy. She found the Sullivans' graves. We visited with their neighbour, Riona and she told us you were here in Ballycotton."

"Riona! A right gossip, but kind-hearted.

"It seems almost too little, too late, doesn't it? It's nice to hear I have family still, but they don't know me, do they? And if Mary did come here and we met, what if she didn't like me? Now that would be awkward …"

Deirdre and Moira just looked at each other. This was not how they planned this meeting would go.

"Won't you give it a lash? It seems worth the risks," Deirdre said.

"Can I think about it? Sleep on it and let you know?"

"Of course! We are headed to Schull this evening but will be back this way in a couple days. Here's our card.

Can we have your number as well?"

Niamh gave her a business card with a photo of the lighthouse painting on it.

"This is a whopper," Deirdre said, indicating the painting. "You have quite a gift as an artist."

"Again, more therapy. I can lose myself in the art and forget that I was a cast-off. But I guess now I have to rewrite my own history. That is going to take some time."

They arrived back in Youghal in time for a light supper with Shannon and Darren. Suki was in bits welcoming Deirdre, as if she'd been gone all year instead of all day.

"You're not thinking of heading out this evening! Stay overnight and get a fresh start in the morning."

"We'll need to call and let Ma know not to expect us tonight, then." Deirdre made the call, and they spent the rest of the evening playing cribbage, hearts, and Jack Change It, and getting to know their own extended family once again.

Chapter 38

Oíche aerach is maidin bhrónach.
A lively night and a sad morning.

—Irish Proverb

They arrived in Schull in time for the lunch hour. With Nuala's roommate from culinary school, Molly Ronan, the resident chef at the inn, Dymphna Gallagher had expanded her menu from breakfast and tea only, to a full-service restaurant. Over a ploughman's lunch, the sisters visited with their ma and filled her in on their latest case.

"That poor child! That poor family!" Dymphna's empathetic bone was buzzing. "It's a good thing the Sullivans are dead and gone or I'd be giving them a piece of my mind!"

"Niamh's not a child any longer, but you're right in one sense, she's been traumatised from these events, which

255

have prevented her from developing as she should, as far as relationships go, and her feelings of self-worth are very low."

"Do you think she'll go to America?" Dymphna asked.

"I hope so. It would be a shame to only get to meet Mary, seeing as John can't travel," Moira said.

"Well, tell me, my girls, how long are you staying this visit?"

"Two days. We thought we'd head back at the end of the week and stop in Ballycotton again to get Niamh's answer."

"I'll take you for as long as I can get you!" Dymphna said with a smile.

That night, while Moira and Deirdre slept peacefully under their mother's roof, Niamh tossed and turned, unable to rest. Her mind was filled with images from her childhood — fleeting glimpses of moments with her siblings, and years under the sharp eye and watchful gaze of Imogen Sullivan. When she finally did doze off, she dreamed she was in a small currach, tethered to a large yacht. Her family of siblings, her ma and da, were in the larger craft looking down at her as she called to them. They smiled and waved, but she remained there in the tiny boat alone, tossed in the wake of the bigger ship as it ploughed a path across the wide ocean.

She awoke in a sweat and glanced at the clock: Three o'clock in the wee hours. She got up and dressed, putting her painter's smock over her head. When she got like this, art was the only thing that soothed. She put a fresh piece of watercolour paper on her work surface and began …

Two hours later she had captured her dream image. Putting it down on the paper got it out of her head at least. And it wasn't a bad rendering, either. She cleaned her brushes and put away her paints, undressed and crawled back under the duvet. She slept deeply until the sound of rain lashing the window woke her at nine o'clock in the morning.

Although it wasn't yet Sunday, her day to visit the Sullivan plot with fresh flowers, she decided to drive to Midleton anyway. No flowers this time. She wasn't in the mood to curry favour, even with the deceased.

The rain was still spitting as she drove into the cemetery, but as she got out and opened her brolly, a ray of sun split the stones. As she walked towards her — what exactly were they to her? Certainly not her parents — the Sullivan graves, she noticed for the first time a grave marker with the name 'Aoibh' nearby. Not Aoibh Collins, of course, but her mother's name triggered a memory — a song floated on the air, and she could almost believe she heard it with her ears as well:

Dilín ó deamhas ó deamhas

Dilín ó deamhas ó dí

Dilín ó deamhas ó deamhas ó deamhas ó

Dilín ó deamhas ó dí

She was on her ma's knee, being bounced up and down, the words of the nursery rhyme keeping time. She had been loved! She knew it, felt it. She didn't need to confront the Sullivans. They had done wrong, but there was nothing to be done about it now but move forward — towards the remains of her family who had finally returned to her.

CHAPTER 39

———

An rud is annamh, is iontach
What is rare is strangest.

—Irish Proverb

"Why don't you leave Suki here with me?" Dymphna said on Saturday morning as her daughters packed up the Mini for the trip back north. "She's such a great watchdog; I could use the comfort of her here."

"Why Ma, has something happened? Have you had any incidents that have caused you to worry?" Deirdre asked.

"No incidents, but being an inn, we are more open to the public than a normal home."

"That's true, but it's never been a problem before. I just wondered why you feel that way now," Deirdre said.

Just then Molly came out to see them off and Deirdre took the opportunity to ask the same question of her.

"Has anything dodgy happened here lately? Ma seems worried …"

"Well sure and there was the incident of the disappearing pie a few days ago, but that's all," Molly said.

"Disappearing pie? What was that about?" Deirdre pressed.

"I set some pies out on the counter in the kitchen before the dinner crowd arrived, then left to set table. When I came back, one of the pies was gone."

"Ma, is that what's worrying you? If you had Suki here, she might just as easily be the culprit stealing the pies!" Moira said.

"You have to admit that it's quite unusual for pies to go missing," Dymphna said.

"I wish you'd said something when we first arrived, we could have looked into it for you. Do you want us to stay another day?" Deirdre asked.

"You know I'd be delirah if you stayed longer, but I don't want to keep you from your business," Dymphna said.

Deirdre looked at Moira, who shrugged. Then they both began unpacking the Mini.

Back inside the inn, Molly approached the sisters with Kayleigh, the part time maid in tow.

"I think you should hear what Kayleigh has to say," Molly began.

"What's the story, Kayleigh?" Deirdre asked.

"I'm scarlet to say, as I was sure I must have misplaced it somewhere …"

"Go on, misplaced what?" Deirdre encouraged.

"A duvet. I was airing out the bedding and had the duvets draped over the open windowsill. Well, the next thing I know, I'm missing one. Sure, and we've got extras, so no guest went cold, but I've looked everywhere for it!" Kayleigh was close to tears. "I know I should have said something to Ms Gallagher, but as I said, I've been trying to find it."

"When did this happen?" Moira asked.

"Two days ago, now."

"I'm sure you're not to blame, Kayleigh. We'll sort this all out," Deirdre said, and Kayleigh smiled and went back to work.

"Thanks for bringing that to our attention, Molly. What do you think is going on?" Deirdre asked.

"Someone playing a prank? Neighbourhood kids?"

"That's a possibility. Do you have something we can use to lure whoever it is to strike again? Pasties maybe? Or biscuits you can leave out on the kitchen counter again?" Deirdre asked the chef.

"I was going to make beef hand pies for lunch."

"That will do. Let me know when they're ready, then

we'll try to catch our thief," Deirdre said.

When Molly left, Moira asked her sister, "Bedding, food, a bit unusual for a thief to target these items, don't you think?"

"Highly unusual. Feel like taking a little drive with me? I was thinking of checking in with the Schull garda station to see if there are any reports of other thefts of this kind."

"Let's go!"

They spoke with young Colin Byrnes, who was manning the desk at the garda station. They had gone to school with Colin and liked to tease him about finally being on the right side of the law, but now they were all business.

"Guard Byrnes, could you tell us if there have been any reports of small-time thefts in the area? Some items seem to be going missing at the inn," Deirdre began.

"I've not had any reports, but I can check the ledger for you. Would you care to wait?" He, too, was being very professional.

"Thank you, sir," Deirdre said.

He was gone about fifteen minutes. "Tadhg Kelly had his car stolen last week. But to be fair, he left it unlocked with the keys in it outside the pub. It was returned to his own drive the next morning, so no harm done."

"Not what we're looking at, but thanks for checking."

"Would you like to make a formal report of theft?"

"Not yet. We may be back, though. It was nice seeing you, Colin," Moira said, and they left.

On the drive back to the inn, they discussed strategies.

"These thefts were done during the day, right? I think we just need to be observant. Do you think it could be an employee?" Moira asked.

"There's only Molly and her sister, Alana, in the kitchen, Kaleigh to help Ma with the rooms, and a busboy. We've known each of them for donkey's years; I can't imagine it's any of them," Deirdre replied.

"What about a gardener? Doesn't Ma have someone to do the mowing and trimming?"

That's mostly in the spring and summer. There's nothing growing now that needs tending," Deirdre said.

It was half-ten when they arrived back at the inn. Dymphna was in her office and Molly and Alana were setting up the dining room for the lunch crowd.

"Are the hand pies done?" Deirdre asked Molly.

"They're in a warming tray on the counter."

"Can you three stay out of the kitchen then, for a bit?"

"We'll be busy in here, for sure."

Deirdre and Moira went into the kitchen and found a place to observe the area unseen by standing in the pantry and looking out the small window in the door.

"How long do you think we should watch?" Moira asked.

"It could be a short time, a long time or nothing could happen at all. We just have to see how it goes."

They waited for forty-five minutes with no sign of any intruders, not even a mouse. As they were both feeling very hungry for those meat pies, they called off the vigil.

"We'll try again at dinner," Deirdre determined.

"Speaking of dinner," Molly said, "I'm making a roast that needs to slow cook. Could one of you run out to the potting shed and get me a bunch of rosemary?"

"I'll go," Deirdre said.

The potting shed had been Deirdre's home-away-from-home when she was still living at the inn. It's where she first became interested in herbal medicine, growing and drying her own herbs. It wasn't used so much in the winter months, but there were still dried herbs hanging for culinary use.

She didn't notice it at first, as the potting table was at the back of the shed, but after cutting a sprig of rosemary, she did a quick turn about the place for nostalgia sake, and saw the corner of a cloth protruding from under the table. Bending down, she realised it wasn't just a rag, but a whole duvet, pushed back underneath. Besides the duvet, she noticed a well-worn suitcase and a pink backpack.

Leaving everything undisturbed, she closed the door of the shed and returned to the kitchen.

"Here's the rosemary. Oh, and I think I've discovered the hideout of our thief."

Chapter 40

An té nach bhfuil láidir, ní mór dó a bheith glic.
He who is weak needs to be clever.

—Irish Proverb

"How do we catch our trespasser?" Dymphna asked, as she, Molly, Alana, Deirdre and Moira met together to discuss the problem.

"One of us can stand watch at the upstairs window that overlooks the garden," Molly suggested. "We can take turns, as it may take a while before she returns."

"She?" Alana asked.

"Well, the pink backpack … I just assumed …"

"Our thief could have stolen the backpack as well," Alana replied.

"How about this," Dymphna proposed. "We make up a nice dinner of Molly's delicious roast beef, colcannon and a few biscuits, put them in a warming box and set it on top of the potting table."

They all just looked at her. Then Moira said, "You want to reward this person for taking your things?"

"I'm guessing it's a runaway. If they know we are here to help and are not angry about the thefts, maybe they'll come clean," Dymphna explained.

"Makes sense. But we should still keep watch, in the event they are more sceptical of our offerings," Deirdre suggested.

The trap was set an hour before the inn guests were due to arrive for their dinner. Moira and Dymphna took the first watch from the upstairs window. They were to signal a sighting to Deirdre downstairs by ringing a bell. Dusk was settling in, and the garden was soon full of shadows.

"It's hard to see anything, Ma. We should have set a light out," Moira said.

"Patience can conquer destiny, my dear."

Just then Moira gave a cry. "There! A shadow … Now I can see the light of a torch inside the shed," Moira said, and she rang the bell.

Deirdre and Molly jumped up from the kitchen table at the sound and raced out the back door. They hadn't quite reached the shed when the door opened and a young girl stood before them holding the warming box, tears streaming down her face.

"You're not angry with me?" She choked out.

"Come inside, child, and eat your dinner where it's warm," Deirdre said.

Once the girl was seated at the kitchen table, Dymphna said, "Go on with you — give the child some space to eat in peace. There's an inn full of guests that are ready for their dinner now."

Alana and Molly left, but Moira and Deirdre stayed.

"What's your name, dear," Dymphna said.

"Caoimhe … Caoimhe Hegarty, ma'am."

"Fiona's daughter? I thought you looked familiar. How's your family getting on after your ma's passing last month?"

"Fine."

"Don't go being a muppet. You're not fine if you're out sleeping in our shed and stealing for your meals. Now what's the story?" Deirdre scolded.

"Don't eat her head off, Deirdre. She'll tell us in her own time. Let the child eat," Dymphna said.

Caoimhe ate quickly, then stood to go. "Thank you for the food. I'll give you back your duvet and be gone. Sorry for all the trouble."

"Stall the ball, girl. You need to tell us what's going on," Deirdre said, and this time Dymphna only nodded.

Caoimhe sighed. "Pa was for sending me up to

Galway to live with Ma's sister when Ma died. Said he couldn't deal with me. But I won't go there. Uncle Brandan is always fluthered and my cousin, Seamus, is a dosser. I said goodbye to Da at the bus station, then had the driver stop and let me off just outside town. I called and told Aunt Gráinne that Da had changed his mind and was keeping me home. That was a week ago, and I've just been getting by on my own."

"Sleeping in our shed and thieving is not getting by young lady. How old are you, anyway? I'm guessing you haven't been to school all week. Now what are we to do with you?" Dymphna asked, not expecting an answer.

"I'm fourteen, and I can work. Couldn't I stay here and help you with the inn?" Caoimhe asked, a hopeful note creeping into her voice.

"Now that's an idea. I could use some help now that Kaleigh has gone to part-time. I'd have to speak with your da, though. Room and board and pocket change for a few hours of work after school?"

A broad grin spread across Caoimhe's face. She jumped up and threw her arms around Dymphna.

"Ma always said you were sound."

"I'm very sorry for your loss, child. Your ma was a good woman, herself," Dymphna said.

Chapter 41

Níl aon tinteán mar do thinteán féin.
There is no place like home.

—Irish Proverb

"Goodbye! Bye! Bye!" It was a veritable party send-off as Moira and Deirdre, minus Suki, headed out the next morning. After consulting with Suki, herself, Deirdre tearfully agreed to a trial separation, letting the dog have an extended holiday.

"Have you heard from Niamh?" Moira asked her sister as they got on the N71. "Is she expecting us?"

"I said we'd be in Ballycotton around half-ten," Deirdre said. "I also let Shannon know we'd like to stay with them tonight. She was disappointed when I said we'd be leaving Suki in Schull."

"Suki does have her fans," Moira laughed.

"This business with Caoimhe — what does it remind you of?" Deirdre began.

"Oh, I don't know … that Ma is an angel?"

"That for sure, but I was thinking that things haven't changed much from the days of the Magdalenes. Young girls are still being cast off by their families and having to choose between one evil and another."

"But it's like Nana Brigid said to me in Glasnevin — we do whatever we can, one soul at a time," Moira replied.

The sisters pulled up outside Niamh's cottage. When they knocked, Niamh opened the door and beckoned them inside.

"I've had some experiences since we last spoke. I believe I'm ready to meet with my sister and brother," she began.

"That's grand! Can you share with us what has happened?" Moira asked.

As Niamh recounted her dream, and her experience in the cemetery — her vivid recollection of her ma singing to her — the sisters were greatly moved.

"Would you like us to contact Mary, or do you wish to do so yourself?" Deirdre asked.

"I think I would like to send her an email. I'll plan to go to the States, but I don't want to travel in the winter. I've got several shows in the area over the next few months and will plan to purchase a plane ticket for April sometime. But meanwhile, I'm hoping we can get to know each other by corresponding and maybe even a phone call."

"That's a sound idea. I'm sure Mary and John will be thrilled to hear from you," Deirdre said. "What do you think, Moira? Moira?"

Moira had turned around in her chair and was staring at the door, which remained firmly closed.

"Sorry, sorry, I just felt like the door had opened and a group of people had just entered …"

Then Moira saw them. She didn't know their names, but knew two of them must be Aoibh and Shay Collins. They were surrounded by six others, all with a family resemblance around the eyes and nose. They were beaming as they gathered around Niamh.

Bad Blood

CHAPTER 42

—

Is ait an mac an saol.
Life is strange.

—Irish Proverb

March 2013

"I miss Suki. Do you think she's having fun at the inn?" Deirdre asked Moira, as the rain bucketed down and there seemed no sign of spring.

"Ma says everyone dotes on her. Especially Caoimhe. I'm not suggesting that Suki has found a new person, but I'm sure she's content and well cared-for."

The doorbell rang taking Deirdre out of her reverie. "I'll get that."

She opened the door and gave a little cry.

"Who is it? What's wrong?" Moira called, already on her way to the door. She arrived to see Deirdre enveloped in a hug from a tall, dark, handsome Italian.

"Giulio! How nice to see you! How long have you been back in Ireland?" Moira asked as Deirdre untangled herself from his fierce embrace.

"I just got here. I couldn't stay away any longer," Giulio said. He kissed Deirdre on both cheeks, then asked, "Is eighteen months a long enough break for you, *cuore mio*? Are you ready to let me back into your life?"

"And how is your mother?" Deirdre replied, ignoring the question.

A cloud passed over his expression. "She is no longer with us."

'Giulio, what do you mean? Has your mother died? What happened?" Deirdre said with great alarm. "But first, come inside. I'll make us tea. It really is good to see you."

Moira and Giulio sat at the kitchen table while Deirdre fussed with the tea service. Giulio began his tale.

"Her broken leg healed just fine, but then she got an infection that set her back a bit. She was getting better, but then my brother arrived —"

"Your brother? I didn't know you have a brother," Deirdre interrupted.

"*Sì*, I did not tell you about him. He is what you call, the black sheep? He left home so many years ago in a quarrel with our father right before papà died. We hadn't heard from Nicola for so long we wondered if he was still alive. Mamma had even hired someone to try to find him — he broke her heart, but he is still her firstborn son, her *tesoro*, her treasure — but no luck.

"Then he came back about six weeks ago. He was very sorry, very caring of her. We asked where he had been all these years, but he just brushed it off. 'Here and there,' was all he would say.

"A few weeks ago, I came home from the market and found mamma at the bottom of the stairs. She had fallen and her neck was broken. Nicola was nowhere around. I called the ambulance, but I knew it was too late. She was gone.

"Now we have just had the reading of her will, and somehow, in the time Nicola has been home, he has been able to get mamma to change her will to leaving all to him, her firstborn. I do not like it. Not the fact that I have only been left a small inheritance, but it's the quiet, hidden way it was done. And then she dies? It is too dark, too mysterious.

"I want to hire Gallagher Investigations to look into mamma's death."

"You think Nicola killed your mother? Pushed her down the stairs to obtain the family fortune?" Deirdre asked.

"I do not know what to think, but I want to know the truth."

"Is Nicola still around?" Moira asked.

"Oh, yes. He has taken over the family home as the Lord of the Manor. I could not live under the same roof, even though he has graciously allowed me to live there still. I have moved into *la pensione* on the grounds. Will you come to Italy with me? Not as *mia ragazza* — unless you want to be! — but as my investigators. Both of you! I am hoping Moira's gifts may also be helpful. Nuala as well, if she wants."

"Haven't the authorities investigated? What did they say about all this?" Deirdre asked.

"*La polizia* have investigated, and concluded it was an accidental death. Nicola has an alibi; he said he was with the vineyard manager in the office. That is several buildings away from the main house, on the other side of *la pensione*. The manager backs up his story."

"You don't believe them," Moira said. It was a statement, not a question. Giulio just looked at the sisters, his eyebrows raised and his dark eyes flashing.

"I know nothing about my brother or what kind of life he has led these past ten years. He has always been hot-tempered. He left home in a fit of anger when papà would not turn over the management of the vineyard to him and instead hired a new manager when the old one retired. Nicola was a big spender back then. He wined and dined women and spent time at the gambling tables. I believe papà didn't trust him with the business he had spent his life building."

Deirdre and Moira looked at each other, but this time, Moira couldn't read what Deirdre was thinking.

"We'll have to discuss this, think about it. We'll talk to Nuala," Deirdre said. "How long are you in Ireland?"

"For as long as it takes to convince you to come back with me."

Chapter 43

—

Eochair feasa foghlaim
Learning is the key to knowledge.

—Irish Proverb

"Where are you staying?" Deirdre asked.

"I'm at a hotel in the city. I've booked it for a week, but I hope it won't take that long for you to decide to help me," Giulio replied. "I've got a few things to do now, but may I take you to dinner tonight?"

"Let's talk tomorrow. We'll need to speak with Nuala, and call Ma to see about Suki. With an open-ended invitation as this is, we'd have to be sure she's okay with keeping Suki indefinitely."

"Alright, I'll call you tomorrow." Giulio kissed Deirdre on each cheek, turned and did the same to Moira and took his leave.

"Well! What do you think about that?" Deirdre asked her sister when he was gone.

"It's come as rather a shock, I must say," Moira said. "I feel like we are becoming an international organisation after our trip to New Zealand last autumn and now this!"

"Is there anything preventing us from going?" Deirdre asked.

"We have no current cases. I was thinking of taking some classes to fill the time. Something like a martial arts class, maybe. After being locked up in Daniel Hobson's shed, I think I'd like to be better prepared for future physical confrontations. But I haven't signed up for anything yet, so that could wait. I'm not sure what Nuala's got on her plate, but I know her catering business has taken off recently, so she may be committed to that."

"Let's get her on the phone, then," Deirdre said.

They made the call, and after explaining the situation, Nuala confirmed that her schedule wouldn't allow her to be out of the country for the next several months.

"Wedding season is coming up! Plus, graduations. This is my busiest time for catering gigs. I've even had to hire several people to help me. As much as I'd love to go with you, I don't see that happening. But I think you both should do it! You may be the only ones who *can* figure out what is going on, if the Italian police have already dismissed it as an accident."

After another call to Dymphna, the sisters were assured they were free and clear to make the trip. Giulio was thrilled. That evening he took both Moira and Deirdre out to dinner.

"I'm so relieved! I know you will solve this mystery. And I am so happy to be able to show you my home, my country. Neither of you have been to Italy before?"

"England, Scotland, The Netherlands, Belgium, America, and as of last autumn, New Zealand. That's the extent of both of our travel experience," Deirdre said. "I'm excited for this opportunity, as well as hopeful we can help you."

All this time, Moira was quiet. Giulio turned to her and asked, "What about you, Moira, are you excited to come to *bellissima Italia?*"

Moira sighed deeply. "I was just thinking, maybe I should just try to contact your mother here, or even Nana Brigid, and ask if it was an accident or not? If an accident, there is no sense is us going, is there?"

Giulio and Deirdre sat in stunned silence for a moment. Then Giulio said, almost in a whisper, "Can you do that?"

"I can try. What's the worst that can happen? Silence?"

"Can I … may I … I would like to be with you when you try," Giulio said.

"That might be a good idea, since I don't have any other connection to your mother, or anything of hers as a token."

"Really? That would be 'grand,' as you say! When would you want to try to … make contact with her?" Giulio's face was lit up with excitement.

"We could try this evening when we get home," Moira suggested.

It seemed like the three rushed through the rest of their meal and soon found themselves seated in the Gallagher's living room.

"I usually try to go to a cemetery or some other quiet, natural spot, but I have received Visitors here at home before, so … if you both could remain quiet and calm, that will help, I guess."

Giulio sat next to Deirdre on the couch and as the silence in the room settled on them, he took hold of her hand. She squeezed it and smiled at him.

Moira closed her eyes and took some deep breaths, then her eyes flew open, and she said, "I don't know your mother's name … that is a good place to start."

"Marcella Marino-Mancuso."

Moira continued her preparations, slowing her

breathing, reaching out her thoughts to the Otherside, blocking out her surroundings, and opening her heart to the departed.

"Marcella Marino-Mancuso, I am reaching out to you on behalf of your son, Giulio. He is worried about you and the manner of your passing. Can you come and let us know if you passed peacefully, or were you hurried out of this world prematurely by someone or something outside of yourself?"

She stopped speaking aloud but continuing to send her thoughts out in an ongoing dialogue with the spirit world. *If your death was at the hands of another, I can help. Giulio wants to see justice done. He is here with me, but he won't be able to see or hear you. You may speak freely, and I will relay to him your message.*

She felt a cool breeze blow through the room. She opened her eyes to see an elegant lady standing before her. She should have asked Giulio for a photograph, but who else could this be but Marcella? Soft curls framed her round face, and her brown eyes sparkled as she greeted Moira.

How lovely to be called upon for a visit! I was just getting used to life on this side and letting go of all that had happened before; but now you are asking me to revisit the scene of my death?

Giulio thinks you were helped along and that your fall was no accident. Is this true?

I was not ready to leave, no. I had so much more I wanted to accomplish! And my son, Nicola had just returned to me.

Nicola, was he with you when you died?

Nicola? No … I had just met with Enzio; we were going through the books for the vineyard. I remember now, I was pointing out some discrepancies … we were upstairs in my office. I was signing some paperwork he had brought me, and he suggested we go down to the vineyard office where he had more receipts that he wanted to show me to verify the purchases. I started down the stairs and the next thing I remember is meeting mamma and papà who passed on so long ago!

Did you fall? Trip? Lose your balance?

Pshht. I could have had a heart attack, for all I know. I'm sorry I can't help you further. How is Giulio? Is he enjoying having his brother home? Are they getting to know one another again? It is so nice that they have each other now that I and their father are both gone. And is that his girl sitting next to him? Deirdre, right? Don't they look lovely together? I'm so glad he found someone to love. He talked all the time about his Irish lass and how much I would love her. I'm happy for them.

Mrs Mancuso—

Marcella. Call me Marcella.

Marcella, did you change your will right before you died?

My will? Heavens no! Why would I do that? Giulio has been by my side this long while, helping to run the vineyard. I encouraged him to go back to school and finish i suoi studi — his studies, and it was meant to be, wasn't it, for that is how he met his bellissima Deirdre! But everything has always been his to inherit, he has been my rock, il mio consigliere e compagno since Nicola left and my Marco passed on. Why do you ask that?

A will has surfaced giving everything to Nicola. Can you tell me where your original will is located?

Mia Volontà? Why, it's where I've always kept it — in il nascondiglio. Ah, look at my boy! Così felice! He can't hear me, you say? Tell him to give Deirdre my pearls. I saved them for his sweetheart, whoever she would be. Is that all now, dear? I must go now; mi papà was about to share with me more of his stories of the war. Take good care of my Giulio … Ciao!

And she was gone.

Chapter 44

—

"Did you see her? What did she say? How did she look?" Giulio was full of questions. He had jumped up from the couch the moment Moira shook herself, stood and stretched.

"She is lovely. I wish we could have meet her before her death. And she loves you, and Deirdre apparently."

"What? What do you mean, she loves me?" Deirdre asked.

Giulio blushed and began to stammer, "I … I may have talked about you a bit to mamma. She was looking forward to meeting you."

"Is that so?" Deirdre had her hands on her hips, but she was smiling. She reached out her hand to him and he

291

took it, sitting back down on the couch next to her.

"What else did she say? Did she tell you who murdered her?" Deirdre turned to Moira, getting to the point.

"I don't think she knows. She said she could have had a heart attack. She didn't say she tripped."

"There was an autopsy. The medical examiner found no evidence of a heart attack or stroke or any other physical ailment that could have caused her to fall," Giulio said. "What did she say about Nicola?"

"He wasn't with her, but Enzio was."

"Enzio! But he is Nicola's alibi! That means they are in this together!" Giulio once again jumped up from where he sat and began pacing the room.

"That does seem to pose a discrepancy in their accounts," Moira said.

Giulio stopped pacing and turned to stare at Moira. "I never told you the manager's name. You called him 'Enzio.' How did you know his name was Enzio?"

"Your mother just told me."

"You are the real deal then. You really do see and hear and talk with the dead! I mean, I believed you, but … but … this is proof. Proof that mamma was really here in this room with me! Moira, you sweet, special, wonderful woman! You have made my heart so happy!"

Giulio swooped Moira up in his arms and swung her around in a circle before setting her back down.

"Should I be jealous?" Deirdre said with a grin.

Giulio ran to her side and took both her hands in his, kissing them several times. "*Carissima!* You as well are special and sweet and wonderful to me! That is why you must come back to Italy with me. I need you. I need you both."

Moira cleared her throat. "Marcella also said she hadn't made another will. Her original left all to you, Giulio."

"Did she say where it is located?"

"Oh, she did … but I didn't quite get what the word was …il nas— something … nascon— I'm sorry. I should have asked her to tell me in English."

"*Il nascondiglio?* It means 'hiding place.' *Compartimento nascosto?* Some sort of hidden compartment?"

"A secret drawer, maybe?" Deirdre guessed.

"The desk drawers were all unlocked. No will was found."

"Could she have meant a different desk? Or a disguised hidden panel?" Moira suggested.

"I don't know, I don't know! This is why I need you to come!" Giulio was becoming more and more agitated.

"Alright, I guess we go to Italy, then!" Deirdre said.

Fortunately, they had all their travel documents in order from their last recent trip abroad and seats were still available on Giulio's flight back at the end of the week. They booked a one-way, not knowing how long it would take to resolve the many questions surrounding Marcella's death. They called Billy, Suki's dog-sitter, and asked him to come in once a week as necessary to water plants. Other than that, they were free to go.

A call to Nuala to update her on their new case prompted Nuala to suggest she could do some digging into Enzio's past and the missing years that Nicola was absent from the family. She promised to keep them updated as to anything she might find.

Their five-and-a half-hour flight had a stopover in Frankfurt, but they were in Florence by seven that evening. Exiting the Amerigo Vespucci Airport, Moira asked if they should flag down a taxi.

"Taxi? No, I left my car here at the long-term parking when I left." Giulio led them to the parking garage and astonished them by stopping at a Maserati GranCabrio.

"This is your car?" Deirdre asked.

"I bought it before I came to Ireland and it was in storage while I was away, but it seems to be running like new since I've been back. You like it?"

"It's nothing like the beat-up VW bus you drove in Ireland ..." Moira observed.

"I loved that bus! But this is nice, too, no?" He opened the passenger door and pulled forward the seat for Moira to get in the back, then gave Deirdre a hand as she slid into the passenger seat. The sun would be setting soon, and the spring temperatures were hovering in the mid-teens Celsius, so they kept the top up, but the speed and dexterity of the machine along the curving roads of the countryside were still breathtaking. As they drove the hour south from Florence, they could still make out the stone and stucco houses dotting the hillsides with their red terracotta roofs providing dots of colour across the still-brown vineyards and fields. About forty-five minutes into the drive, Giulio turned off the SS2 onto a smaller side road.

"The sign said twenty-three kilometres still to Siena. Where are you taking us, signore Mancuso?" Moira asked.

"Are you worried I am kidnapping you, signorina Gallagher?" Giulio laughed. "I say I am from Siena because no one knows where is Casole d'Elsa. Saying I am from Siena is much easier and requires little explanation. It is about the same distance from Firenze, we have approximately fifteen kilometres to go."

A short time later, Giulio pointed out Deirdre's window and said, "Look! That is our destination."

On the crest of a small hill sat a two-story stone cottage with a brown terracotta roof. Four windows facing front on the upper story held window boxes overflowing with geraniums. It was a solid yet welcoming structure. They turned into a gravel, cypress-lined drive and could catch glimpses through the trees of the vineyards extending out on either side.

"This is *la pensione*. The main house is about a kilometre further down the road. We offer the cottage as a bed and breakfast throughout the year, but with Nicola in the main house, I have blocked out three rooms for us to use here. I hope you will be comfortable."

"It's lovely, Giulio. But I had no idea you — your family — were so … well off," Deirdre said.

"Does that make a difference?"

"Not at all!"

Chapter 45

Imíonn an tuirse is fanann an tairbhe.
Tiredness goes away and the benefit remains.

—Irish Proverb

After putting her suitcase in her assigned room, Deirdre knocked on Moira's door.

"Avanti!"

"Trying out your beginner Italian, eh?" Deirdre said as she walked in. Moira's room was a mirror image of her own: burnt sienna floor tiles, high ceilings encircled by crown moulding, two single beds with inviting duvets, a tall, wooden armoire and an over-stuffed chair upholstered in a colourful floral design. A bouquet of fresh flowers sat in a crystal vase on the side table. Deirdre sat in the chair and watched Moira unpack her clothes into the armoire.

"My room is blue, but I really like this peach-colour that complements the floor tiles."

"Want to switch?"

"I don't want to switch! I'm just noting the differences. And I'm gobsmacked that this is what Giulio comes from," Deirdre said.

"Well, it's no longer his, now, is it? It's Nicola's."

"For the time being. You said Marcella didn't change her will. We've got to find that original and prove the new one is a fake, among other things."

"You said when we arrived that his family background doesn't make any difference. Did you mean it? Does it change anything of how you feel towards him?" Moira questioned.

"I don't think so … I care about him very much, and the break we had has made me feel that even more strongly. I missed him! But do I love him? I have never felt that way about anyone else I've dated, but I don't know if it's love. And sometimes he is so annoying! That was quite presumptuous of him to come and give us only a few days to upend our lives and follow him to Italy! But when we were in the room with you as you experienced the visitation with his mother, I feel like his attitude and understanding of what we do was dramatically altered when it became so personal.

"Remember how he was always telling us what we were doing was "too dangerous" and I should follow a path in law? He sees the importance of our work now like he never has before. That is important to me, to be able to feel that support from those I love. And just for argument's sake, what if I do love him? What then? His home is here, mine is in Ireland. I could never leave Ma and my sisters!"

"You don't have to decide now, but it is something to consider," Moira agreed.

A knock at the door and Giulio's voice: "Anyone home? Who wants dinner?"

Moira opened the door, and they followed him back down to the driveway.

"There's a little trattoria down the hill — we passed it on the way in — that is a favourite. Come let me treat you to a humble country meal."

It was after nine in the evening, but the eatery was bustling with customers. After giving some recommendations, Giulio ordered for them: *Prosciutto e melone, Gnocchi di patate alla pomarola, Insalata rucola.*

"Just something light, then leave room for *il dolce? Panna cotta* or *tiramisù?*"

Deirdre laughed. "I'll let you know after the gnocchi and salad if I've got room."

Over coffee they discussed what the plan was for the coming days.

"I will take you to the big house tomorrow to meet

Nicola. As I said, he is being very cordial. I told him I was inviting some of my Irish friends to stay for a while and he is excited to meet you. He knows nothing of Gallagher Investigations, or my determination to get to the truth of mamma's death."

"We will play the tourists then," Deirdre said.

"I'm looking forward to meeting Enzio. I often can get a vibe of the person from just a first meeting," Moira said.

"I will give you a tour of the winery operations as a reason to meet Enzio. He has been with us about five years. The manager papà hired right before his passing moved to Crete to be closer to his wife's family. It took us quite a few months before we were able to hire Enzio. In the meantime, I got an in-depth experience running the operations on my own."

"What is he like?" Deirdre asked.

"Enzio? Charming. A people-pleaser. He is a hard worker though; I'll give him that. You will decide for yourselves tomorrow."

Tomorrow arrived sooner than the sisters would have liked after the long flight, late dinner and even later conversation. Giulio had warned he'd get them for breakfast at 8 a.m., and they stumbled down still sleepy-eyed. It was served a la carte in the dining room of *la pensione*. Lucia, the live-in cook, was there to oversee the breakfast service and chatted with the sisters, wanting to practice her English.

"How long your holiday? You will visit Pisa, yes? And Firenze? Roma is far, but you go?"

"That would be lovely. We aren't sure yet how long we'll be here. We hope to see all those places while we are here," Deirdre said. "And your English is *molto bene!*"

At that encouragement, Lucia erupted into a stream of Italian that was completely lost on the two Irish women with their secondary-school proficiency. Smiles and nods got them through the breakfast chatter, then they hustled up to their rooms to get properly dressed and ready to go to the 'big house.'

It was an apt description. *La Vigna Mancuso* had to be at least 380 square metres of vine-covered stone. Large terracotta urns of topiary lined the cobblestoned courtyard.

Giulio sounded the knocker on the massive wooden door. Their approach must have been monitored for it was opened immediately by a man in his late thirties.

"Giulio! So, these are your Irish ladies! *Benvenuti a casa mia!* Come in, come in! How was your flight?"

"Moira, Deirdre, this is my brother, Nicola; Nicola, meet Moira, and Deirdre."

Nicola took each of their hands in turn and gave the traditional cheek kisses. He slapped his brother on the back and ushered them into an intimate living room dominated by a massive fireplace that could hold all four of them standing upright inside of it.

"Sit down, and tell me all about yourselves," Nicola began.

"Our flight was smooth and uneventful; thank you for asking. We met Giulio in Dublin when he was at the university. We have become good friends," Deirdre said.

"Good friends, yes, *very* good friends, indeed!" Nicola said with a wink. "I can certainly see the allure; I have never been to Ireland, but if all your women are so lovely …"

Deirdre coloured and for once, had no words. Moira took up the narrative. "I have always wanted to see Italy. You and Giulio are very generous and kind to host us."

"You are most welcome to stay as long as you like. I don't know as you need to stay in *la pensione*, though. There is plenty of room here and it would be my pleasure to host."

"The pensione is charming and quite comfortable," Deirdre assured him.

"*Bene.* And what are your plans for today? I would love to show you around our little corner of paradise. Perhaps if Giulio would like some special time with *la sua fidanzata*, I could interest her fair sister in an *escursione?*"

Now it was Moira's turn to colour, but she didn't answer. Nicola continued. "I am having a few friends in for dinner tomorrow evening if you would care to join us?"

"Friends? Who would that be, Nicola?" Giulio questioned.

"Ah, friends is a strong term. Acquaintances, maybe. Potential investors. I have plans for expansion and am looking for new partners."

"Is that so? What kind of plans?"

"Come tomorrow and you will see! Now, I must see to a few things but make yourselves at home and I hope you have a wonderful first day in *bella Italia!*"

Nicola air-kissed Deirdre's cheeks, then kissed not only Moira's cheeks but bent over and kissed her hand as well. Then with a '*ciao*,' he left them.

"Well, that was interesting," Giulio remarked. "What is he up to?"

"Perhaps we could see the vineyard now, and meet Enzio?" Moira asked.

"*Sì, bene.* We will go now."

Back in the Maserati, Giulio turned to ask Moira, "What is your first impression of my brother?"

"He is definitely hiding something. And he is very cordial — almost *too* cordial. I'm not quite use to all this kissing."

Giulio laughed. "That is just the Italian way. He did seem very attentive to you though. Watch yourself!"

Chapter 46

*Ní bhíonn uasal ná íseal, ach thuas seal
thíos seal*
Noble and poor are both up and down a while.

—Irish Proverb

"Enzio, I'd like to introduce you to my friends, Moira and Deirdre Gallagher. They'll be staying in *la pensione* for a few days. Moira, Deirdre, this is Enzio Esposito, manager of *Vigneti Mancuso*."

"*Piacere,*" Enzio said, extending his hand to the women.

"*Piacere,*" Deirdre replied.

"I'm going to show them around the operations. Is there anything special you'd like to let us know about before the tour?" Giulio asked Enzio.

"A shipment is boxed ready to go out today. The transport should be arriving soon."

"Where is it headed?"

"The usual … *ristoranti a* Pisa, Firenze, Siena …" Enzio waved his arm in a vague gesture encompassing the surrounding area.

"*Grazie,* Enzio."

The man bowed slightly, then turned and went back into the office of the stone building they had entered. Guilio directed them to a door on the far side of the foyer where they'd met Enzio. Deirdre opened the door and was confronted with a long, steep staircase.

What they had thought was a small stone building was only the entrance to the cellars, stretching on and on through rooms containing wooden aging barrels, stainless steel processing vats and row upon row of bottled wines.

"This is amazing! How long have you been in this business?" Deirdre asked Giulio.

"Nicola and I are the twentieth generation of Mancuso vintners. Our family has been in this business for five hundred years," Giulio replied, a hint of pride in his voice. "It is a relatively small operation, but we are all organic; we have a small olive oil business as well. Our wines and oils are grown, produced and bottled right here."

"I had no idea! I thought you wanted to be an archaeologist. Isn't that what you were studying in Israel and then in Ireland?" Deirdre asked.

"Archaeology is my little hobby. It is my interest. But my heart is here in the vineyard. Mamma indulged me and encouraged me to take my studies, but she had always hoped that I would return and establish the next generation of Mancuso vintners."

"This seems like it would be such a huge operation for one family to run," Moira said.

"During certain times of the seasons we hire more local help — the harvest is an especially busy time. But it is manageable."

After the tour the three returned to the pensione where Lucia had set out her homemade biscotti and coffee in the lounge. As they nibbled and sipped, they discussed what their next move would be.

"I need to search again mamma's apartment for the real will," Giulio said. "It must be when Nicola is out, though …"

"Can we check to see if he is out now?" Moira asked.

"Maybe we can use his attentions towards Moira to create an opportunity," Deirdre said. "You could tell him you are taking me out to lunch so we can get reacquainted. He will, of course, ask about Moira, and you can suggest he entertain her for a few hours? Then instead of going to lunch, you and I can go check out the rooms."

"I'm not feeling very comfortable with that idea," Moira said.

"Oh, come on, Mo, take one for the team! What could possibly happen?"

Moira wrinkled her nose but said nothing.

After making the call to Nicola, Giulio said, "For having just met him, you seem to know my brother quite well. He will be waiting for us in front of the big house and will take Moira to lunch."

Moira sighed. "Fine. I'll go up and get changed."

When she returned, the three drove to the main house once again where Nicola was indeed waiting. Deirdre and Giulio watched Nicola's Lamborghini drive away with Moira in the passenger seat, then they drove Giulio's car around the back of the villa out of sight should Nicola return before they were finished. They had agreed to text Moira when they completed their search so she could stall if necessary.

"It's fortunate that Nicola has kept all the staff on, as every one of them loved mamma and thus are loyal to me as well. We will not be questioned."

Entering the villa through the back, Giulio led the way up to the second-floor apartment that had been his mother's private domain.

"You check the bedroom and closet, I'll go through her sitting room and office," Giulio instructed. "Remember, it could be hidden somewhere not obvious. I have no knowledge of any secret, hidden panels or trick drawers, so try anything — loose floorboards, unusually placed items."

They worked quickly but methodically, leaving things as they were, appearing untouched. After an hour they regrouped.

"Anything?" Giulio asked.

Deirdre just shook her head. Giulio sighed. "Now what?"

"Switch places? Maybe you will see something I did not, and vice versa."

It seemed they were at it for hours when they still came up empty-handed. As they stood in the centre of Marcella's office, Deirdre turned a full circle, noting the bookcase lining one wall.

"Did you take out the books to check for a hidden panel?" she asked.

"That is what took the longest time! There is nothing."

Running her hands along the shelves, she noted the titles.

"Was your mother a big reader? I see many books on wines, agriculture, gardening, but also many works of classic literature," Deirdre observed.

"She read to us as children and instilled in me a love of literature, *sì*."

"*Il Piacere* by Gabriele D'Annunzio ... *Il Principe*

by Niccolò Machiavelli … *Divina Commedia* by Dante Alighieri … *La Coscienza di Zeno* by Italo Svevo … these I can understand having a place of honour on her shelves. But here — it's curious there are also titles in English, many of them concerning World War Two."

Deirdre pulled them off the shelf as she read: "*This Has Happened: An Italian Family in Auschwitz, The English Patient* —"

"*Sì, sì,* she had much interest in World War Two. Nonno, her father, was a prisoner of war in Wietzendorf. But we can discuss this later; Nicola could return at any time."

Just then a text came through from Moira: *We are returning.*

"We must go! I hear a car in the drive!" Giulio said with some urgency.

Before leaving, Deirdre grabbed *The English Patient* and *This Has Happened* from off the shelf, then followed Giulio out the door. Nicola was at the bottom of the staircase as they began their descent.

"Ah! You are back soon from your lunch?" Nicola said in surprise. "I didn't see your car out front."

"I drove around back to show Deirdre the view from the terrace," Giulio said.

"Then I was craving something to read at bedtime. I

forgot to bring a book with me — I'm a voracious reader — so Giulio offered to let me borrow one." She held up the volumes. "I couldn't decide which to start so chose these two. Perhaps Moira would like one. Speaking of Moira, how was *your* lunch?"

"*Meravigliosa!* Your sister is a delightful companion, a gifted conversationalist. She wanted to return to the trattoria you went to last evening. I just dropped her off at *la pensione* to freshen up."

"Ah, well I will join her there, then, *ciao!*" Deirdre said as she and Giulio hurried past him.

"Phew, a close one!" Giulio said as they got in the Maserati. "That was quick thinking on the reading material."

"As was your response about showing me the view. I can't wait to get Moira's take on the outing," Deirdre replied. "I would never describe my sister as a gifted conversationalist!"

Back at the pensione they found Moira sipping an espresso from the machine in the lounge.

"I checked the room but when you weren't there, I decided to wait for you here so I could hopefully catch Giulio as well," she said. "Find anything? What have you got there?"

"Decoys to explain our appearance at the house. And we were unsuccessful in finding the will," Deirdre replied.

"Now what is this we hear from Nicola that you are a brilliant conversationalist? Nicola was quite impressed with you."

Moira blushed but dismissed the compliment. "I merely asked him a lot of questions about himself and got him talking. Most people like to listen to themselves talk. I encouraged that in Nicola, thus diverting the conversation away from myself."

"Did he ask you what you did for a living? That was the one thing I was afraid of and wondered what you would say. We hadn't talked about it ahead of time," Deirdre said.

"I was worried about that as well, and he did ask. I played up the family history angle; I said we had a business where we helped people with researching their family history questions."

"Nicely done, Moira!" Giulio said.

"Bang on, Mo!" said Deirdre.

Just then Moira and Deirdre's mobiles pinged with a message. It was from Nuala: *check business email.*

Giulio directed them to a computer station set up in the corner of the lounge for guests. They signed in and Deirdre read aloud the message:

Greetings all, hope you are well. I've been busy, and with a bit of help from Inspector Keating, have discovered a few things.

Nicola was arrested eight years ago for robbery. He spent a year in a prison in Milan, then was transferred to Gorgona island prison off the coast of Livorno. He was released from there three months ago after completing his seven-year sentence.

On Gorgona, he shared a cell with one Enzio Esposito for the first year, as Enzio was finishing his sentence and was released five years ago. Both were assigned to work in the prison vineyard.

I don't have the details of his arrest or specifics of his crime at this time, but I felt it was important to get this information to you, especially the prior connection between Nicola and Enzio.

Hope you are well. Watch yourselves, N

"Very interesting, no?" Giulio said.

"Did you know about this previous connection between the two?" Deirdre asked.

"I did not know. I *did* know that Enzio had been in prison. He had to show his prison release papers during the employment process. But with his experience in the prison vineyard, he was a huge asset for us. It is very difficult to find workers, especially at the management level, who are experienced vintners. But at no time did he hint that he knew Nicola."

"It is interesting that he showed up at your door with these qualifications soon after leaving prison," Moira said. "Do you think Nicola sent him? Perhaps they have been together in some sort of plan all along."

"The meeting tomorrow evening will be very interesting. I hope you both will plan to attend with me."

"We'll be there," Deirdre said.

"Now I will let you rest and read your books. In the morning, we will take a break, and I will give you a taste of Italy. We will drive into Siena, and I will show you that *bella città*."

There were no complaints from Moira or Deirdre on that plan and they both looked forward to the adventure.

CHAPTER 47

—

Bíonn blas ar an mbeagán
A little tastes best.

—Irish Proverb

The drive the following morning was short — forty-five-minutes and then the mediaeval city came into view.

"Oh! It really is the colour of sienna!" Moira remarked.

"The city centre is pedestrian traffic only; we must park outside the city and take an escalator to the top of the hill."

When they arrived at the escalators they were 'temporaneamente fuori servizio,' which meant they had to walk the almost 400 steps to the top. Once they arrived, they found a café and rested their feet and quenched their parched throats.

"Now, are you ready to do a little walking to explore Siena?" Giulio said with a wink.

Moira groaned, but Deirdre said, "Let's go!"

Tickets to the Torre del Mangia were already sold out, but they were okay with that, as the climb to the top was another 400 steps. Instead, they went inside the Siena Cathedral, which was breathtaking. As they continued to explore the city, they came across a bookshop and decided to browse. Most of the titles were in Italian, but Moira found an English guidebook that looked promising containing the local area they hoped to explore.

"Look here!" Deirdre said. She was standing in front of a section marked *Seconda Guerra Mondiale* — World War Two. She held out a slim volume. "I recognised the author's name. This is one of the books I saw on your mother's bookshelf!"

"'Corrie ten Boom,'" Guilio read. "*Sì*, it is one of mamma's favourites from the Nazi concentration camp victim. She read many of these memoirs to get a feeling of what her father went through in the war."

"*Il Nascondiglio*." Moira read the Italian translation of the title. "That is the same word your mother used when she said where her will was located."

The three looked at one another.

"We must get back right away and search your

mother's rooms again!" Deirdre said.

"We'll stop at the big house first, *sì*. If Nicola is out, we will search."

"Even if he's home, I have with me the book I borrowed. I can say I have decided to swap it out for something else," Deirdre added.

"*Carissima*! You are always thinking! And you are always prepared. But now, we'll have lunch here in Siena before we head back."

He steered them to a restaurant a few steps from the Piazza del Campo that he had been hoping to show them: Antica Osteria da Divo.

"The restaurant is located inside Etruscan-era tombs. I thought, you know, with Moira's affinity for the dead …" He shrugged. The sisters laughed and Moira said, "By all means, sounds fascinating!"

Once inside the restaurant they went down two levels and were seated in a candlelit niche. Giulio informed them that cinerary urns holding the ashes of the dead would have been placed in crevices in the walls.

"Can you sense the dead here, Moira?" he asked in all sincerity.

"It is only a room now, no spirits are present but those of the living, as far as I can tell," she replied.

Although they all had appetites, they were too excited

at their discovery of the possible meaning of '*Il Nascondiglio*' in regard to Marcella's will to indulge in several courses, so ordered from the first course menu only. Deirdre had the risotto carnaroli with saffron, Moira chose crepes with sea bass and Giulio went with paccheri pasta with tomatoes and olives. It was hard to leave such a beautiful city only partially explored, but Giulio promised they would return.

Driving back to Casole d'Elsa, Moira observed, "You know, even if we find the original will, it doesn't change anything. The will Nicola presented is dated after it and would supersede it, correct?"

"True. We still need to prove the new will is a fake," Giulio said. "But one step at a time. First, we find mamma's will."

Upon arriving at the house, they learned that Nicola was down at the vineyard office with Enzio, so all three quickly went up the stairs and entered Marcella's rooms. Deirdre went to the bookcase. She pulled *Il Nascondiglio/The Hiding Place* off the shelf and handed it to Giulio. He opened the cover and let out a cry. The inside had been hollowed out to reveal a hiding place within *The Hiding Place*. Nestled in the space was a folded piece of paper. Taking it out,

Giulio read: *Le Ultime Volontà e il Testamento di Marcella Marino-Mancuso.*

"This is it! *Amore*, you've found it!" Giulio swept her up into his arms, crushing the paper and book between them.

"Moira's right, though. It's only a start. But we're on the right track. We need to find proof that the new will is not authentic," Deirdre said.

"I believe Enzio is the key. Marcella said she was with him signing paperwork before she fell. Could he have slipped the will in among other papers and she signed not realizing what it was?" Moira asked Giulio.

"That is hard to believe, mamma was such a good businesswoman. But she had been slipping mentally lately … I was going to take her to *il suo medico* — her doctor — to see if her medications were affecting her badly."

"What is your status concerning the business now that Marcella is gone? Does Nicola have complete control of that as well?" Deirdre asked.

"If that had been in the will, it would have been a red flag that it was a fake. I am listed as a full partner with mamma in the business. That came to me from papà's will. She would not be able to change that, only giving over her shares to Nicola, making him equal partner with me. Which is why I was so surprised when he announced the visitors for dinner tonight. He had made no mention of the meeting to me."

"Let's get this document safely back to the pensione before Nicola shows up here. We have some time before we need to return for dinner," Deirdre suggested.

"*Andiamo!*" Giulio replied.

Chapter 48

─────

Is fearr an tsláinte ná an táinte
Health is better than wealth.

—Irish Proverb

Giulio knocked at Deirdre's door and found Moira there as well, waiting for him. It was a lovely evening, so they decided to walk the half-kilometre to the big house, arriving just in time for the *aperitivo*.

They were ushered into the living room where wines and other *aperitivi* lined a table against one wall. Nicola was there giving instructions to a young man tending the bar. He rushed over to greet them with the traditional cheek kissing, then took Moira by the hand and escorted her to a seat.

"What can I bring you to drink, *bella* Moira?" He asked, bending over her hand to kiss it once again.

"A glass of wine is fine," she said. "You choose something nice."

Giulio went to the bar and got drinks for himself and Deirdre. There were two other gentlemen in the room and Nicola made introductions.

"Let me introduce my guests: Antonio Carbone, Francesco Moretti, this is *mio fratello*, Giulio, and his guests from Ireland, Moira and Deirdre. Tony and Franco are interested in helping us take *Vigneti Mancuso* to the next level."

"And what exactly is 'the next level,' gentlemen?" Giulio asked.

"*Agriturismo*, of course!" Antonio exclaimed. "We'll have tourists coming here from all over to sample your wines, try a little of your organic *olio d'oliva* on your freshly baked bruschetta. They pay to see your barrels and vats, sip a little *vino*, then spend a night or two in your expanded and renovated *pensione*."

"All the vineyards are doing it now, and it has the potential to bring in more income than that of the wines and oils you produce," added Francesco.

"I find it hard to believe *all* the vineyards are doing it, and that we are the last holdouts. Papà was against the idea. That is what you two fought over ten years ago, wasn't it? He wanted to keep things small, local, manageable," Giulio directed to his brother.

"Papà isn't here anymore, is he? He lived in the dark

ages. We need to keep up with the times, brother."

Dinner was announced and the party moved into the dining room. There was a lovely caprese salad at each place setting. The ladies were seated, then the men took their seats. After a *'buon appetito'* from Nicola, all began to eat, The talk of *agriturismo* faded into the background and polite conversation with one's neighbour was the rule. Deirdre was seated across from Giulio with Nicola to her right. When the next course was brought out — a creamy lemon risotto with fennel and parmesan — she asked Nicola, "Have you travelled widely through Italy? Can you tell me, what are the 'must-sees' in your *bella Italia?*"

An innocuous question, but it caused Nicola to pause and redden. Then he replied, "I remember some wonderful family holidays in Venice, Capri, Cinque Terre. Anywhere you go will be a memorable adventure, I'm sure."

"I would love to visit Milan and see Da Vinci's *Last Supper*. Have you been there?"

Again, a pause; this time he furrowed his brow and stared into Deirdre's eyes before saying, "I have not seen *The Last Supper*, no."

"I'm glad you mentioned Cinque Terre. I'm thinking we should rent a car so as not to inconvenience Giulio further. I'd like to travel up the coastline, beginning in Livorno."

Nicola choked out a cough and said, "If you will excuse me a moment." He stood and left the table, exiting the room. Deirdre looked across the table at Giulio and raised her eyebrows. He raised his shoulders slightly in a question.

Nicola soon returned and announced the next course, pork ragù over creamy polenta. Dishes were cleared and when he returned to his seat, he turned to Francesco on his right and began a conversation. Deirdre was left to savour the delicious dish in silence.

After the cherry crostata was brought in, Giulio once again turned the conversation to the subject of agritourism. Addressing no one in particular, he noted, "We already have a pensione that does a steady business all year 'round. What would you have us do more?"

Tony took up the question. "You must include tours of the vineyard, the wine-making process, a tasting centre. These kinds of packages are where the money lies."

"And what do you and Francesco bring to the table in this process?"

Nicola jumped in to explain, "We don't have the capital at this point to outfit the operations to accommodate visitors. We'd need to build a tasting room and expand the pensione. As it is now, we can only accommodate four or five parties. This would be a wise investment that would pay for itself in a very short time."

"And do you have numbers for all this? Have you checked with other enterprises that are moving in this direction? I have heard that as many licences that are taken out for *agriturismo* are cancelled one or two years later."

"This is not the time to discuss. You will meet with Tony and Frank and I after our dinner. I don't want to bore the ladies with talk of business."

"Oh, I find this all fascinating! Don't mind us, we can always learn from you businessmen," Deirdre said, with a self-deprecating smile and flutter of her eyelashes.

It was going on two o'clock in the morning when dinner and discussions had ended, and Giulio walked Moira and Deirdre back to the pensione.

"I think you rattled Nicola's cage there during our *primo* course, Deirdre. I didn't hear what you were saying …" Giulio said, taking hold of her hand.

"I just happened to drop Milan and Livorno into the conversation about Italian travel spots," Deirdre said.

"Ah! So now his suspicions are aroused. Perhaps he thinks we know something?"

"It's important that we have a talk with Enzio before Nicola has a chance to warn him," Moira said.

"I agree. We shall talk to him in the morning," Giulio said.

"It is already morning," Deirdre said with a laugh.

CHAPTER 49

—

Moladh luath agus cáineadh mall
Early praise and delayed criticism

—Irish Proverb

While Moira and Deirdre were readying themselves for the day, Deirdre got a text from Nuala.

Dug up some info on Enzio that I thought you might be able to use. Ma helped me get some genealogical data. Those records are a bit trickier to find than the Irish. His father died in an accident when Enzio was young. He was raised an only child by his mother, Gabriella Ricci-Esposito. She died when he was in his early twenties. Hope you're having a Grand Adventure!

A knock at the door. "*Buongiorno!* Ready for a special surprise?"

They opened the door to Giulio who stood there

with a huge grin on his face. "Lucia wanted to give you a special breakfast this morning. She has heard about the 'full Irish' breakfasts and wanted you to feel at home. Here in *la pensione* it is not possible for her to make a big meal, only the biscotti, cornetto and other pastries and caffè. We are invited to the big house for her sausage and egg strata. Come! You will enjoy!"

Once again, they walked over to the main house, enjoying the cool spring sunshine.

It was a feast indeed: sweet cornettos with a variety of fillings, creamy yogurt with fresh fruit, and in place of honour, a delectable egg dish with layers of sausage, zucchini, peppers, onions, spinach and cheese.

"This should last us all day!" Deirdre commented as they ate heartily.

While they ate, a letter was brought to the table for Giulio.

"This was dropped off this morning for you, *signore*," Lucia said, handing Giulio a business-sized envelope with his name on it and the address of *Vigna Mancuso*.

Using his bread knife, Giulio sliced open the envelope and removed a single piece of paper. As he read, a furrow appeared on his brow.

"Bad news?" Deirdre asked.

"*Sì*, no …" Giulio looked up and said, "It is from a man

named Alessandro DeLuca. He is the private investigator that mamma hired to find Nicola these many years ago. He said he read about mamma's passing and has been struggling with himself whether to contact me or not. He has decided he cannot have it weigh on his conscience anymore.

"Mamma hired him four years ago when she despaired of Nicola returning home on his own. This signore DeLuca says that he did find Nicola, in prison on Gorgona Island. He visited him and Nicola paid him to not tell mamma where he was. He says Nicola was embarrassed and said he didn't want his family to know what had become of him.

"He accepted the payment and swore he wouldn't tell. He reported to mamma that he was not able to find Nicola. But now that he has learned of Nicola's recent return home and the subsequent accidental death of signora Mancuso, he felt he must come forward. He did not want to be a part of something that might prove to be an unnatural death after all."

"Does he say why he thinks Marcella's death could have been unnatural?" Moira asked.

"No, but he has met with Nicola and has researched his background in his search for him. He says he was arrested for robbing a liquor store to pay for gambling debts.

Nicola was in a gang that worked together for a series of robberies. Nicola was the getaway driver. He feels money is important to Nicola and worried when he heard Nicola had inherited from his mother's death so soon after getting released from prison. He doesn't trust him and warns that we shouldn't trust him as well."

"Well, that answers one question I've had. Why didn't the hired detective find out about Nicola when Nuala was able to discover his past so quickly?" Deirdre said.

"*Buongiorno!* How is everyone this *bella giornata?*" Nicola strolled into the dining room and Giulio hastily tucked the letter into his pocket.

"Grand!" Deirdre returned, matching his exuberance.

"And what is the itinerary for today? Can I interest anyone in an excursion to Pisa? Or perhaps you would prefer a less *sito turistico?* For another thirty minutes of driving, you could see Orvieto — *molto affascinante. Bella* Moira, perhaps you would go with me, and we can allow Giulio and his lady to spend the day together?"

"We are all three going to Firenze today. I have already purchased the priority access tickets to the Uffizi."

"Some other time, then, *bella* Moira?" He lifted her hand to his lips.

"Thank you, that would be nice," Moira replied.

Nicola grabbed a cornetto off the table and sauntered

out once more. When he was gone, Moira whispered, "Priority access to the Uffizi?"

"I saw how uncomfortable you were about having lunch with Nicola; I couldn't let you spend four hours in his car and another who-knows-how-many touring the underground hollows of Orvieto with him."

"I appreciate your consideration, but underground hollows actually do sound *molto affascinante,*" Moira laughed.

"Do you want me to call him back?" Giulio asked.

"That's okay; maybe another time, as I said."

"What about our chat with Enzio? Are we not going there this morning," Deirdre asked.

"*Sì.* We will go there before we head to Firenze. And after I purchase the priority access tickets …"

Thirty minutes later they drove into the vineyard office car park. Enzio stepped outside to meet them as they exited the car.

"*Buongiorno, signore.* What can I do for you today?"

"We had a few questions, if you don't mind. Perhaps inside?" Giulio indicated the office door.

They all trooped in, and Enzio found seats for them

all in the small space, then sat behind the desk. "Now, what is it you need?"

They hadn't rehearsed ahead of time exactly what they would say, but Giulio got right to the point.

"Did you learn of *Vigneti Mancuso* from Nicola when you were in prison together in Gorgona?"

Enzio's mouth opened but nothing came out. He then spluttered, "Whatever do you mean? Signore Mancuso knew I was newly out of prison when he hired me. Why do you mention this now?"

"I know you were in prison; that is not the issue. I have only recently learned that you knew my brother, Nicola, there and it seems such a *grande coincidenza* that you showed up here straight away when we needed a manager. Was the scheme to disinherit me planned from the beginning? And did you murder my mother to accomplish that?"

"No, signore! Your mother's death was *un incidente*."

"That may well be, but I also know that you were not with Nicola when mamma fell, and that you *were* with mamma in her upstairs office right before she fell."

"How can you know this? There was no one else there to witness her fall!"

Immediately, he realised what he had said. "I mean, *la polizia* have the full report. I was with Nicola here in this office."

"If it wasn't murder, if mamma truly fell, you would only be facing the lesser charge of fraud in tricking her to sign a new will. For that is what you were doing in her office that morning, was it not?"

Enzio stood, looking wildly around the office, as if searching for an escape route. Then he looked fixedly at Giulio. "You have no proof of this. You are only guessing. I don't have to take this. I will talk to Nicola — he will see to it."

All Giulio had was this bluff, for he couldn't reveal his source as the deceased Marcella's spirit. He looked over at Moira, whom he noticed, had taken on the same faraway expression she had when she was conversing with that very spirit.

"Moira?" he asked.

"Enzio, there is someone here from whom you may have to 'take it.' Your mamma, Gabriella Ricci, has a few words to say."

Enzio's eyes narrowed. "You have been looking into *mia famiglia*? Mamma has been gone these many years. What is the meaning of this?" He paused, lifted his head, sniffed. "What is that smell? What trickery is this?"

"I don't know what you mean," Giulio said.

"Mamma's *profumo*. I'd know it anywhere. It was her special scent: *Cachet* by Prince Matchabelli. I opened it once and spilled it all over the floor … Mamma?" Enzio fell heavily back into the chair.

There was a whirring in the air, as if a small tornado had descended on the room. Papers were lifted and swirled about, the window rattled, the overhead light swayed. The noise became deafening.

"Are you ready to listen to your mother now, Enzio?" Moira said calmly as she sat amidst the whirlwind.

"*Sì, sì*, yes! Make it stop!" he shouted, covering his ears.

The wind died down and calm descended.

"Your mother is saying, '*Gigi, I am so disappointed in you. I did not raise you like this. Your papà left me, and I did my best, but you are not the boy I raised who was so thoughtful, kind and helpful. Do you remember when our neighbours, la famiglia Romano, lost everything in the fire at Natale and there would be no presents for le bambine? You sold your eggs all through dicembre and bought a toy for each of them. What happened to that boy?'*"

Moira continued related the words of the spirit. "'*Tell these people the truth. Face the consequences of your actions so I can be proud of you once again. Now I must leave, but I am always near and always watching over you.*'"

Enzio slumped forward and put his head in his hands. "No one but mamma ever called me 'Gigi,'" He whispered.

"Why did she call you 'Gigi?" Giulio asked, quite puzzled.

"My first name is Luigi, but I never liked it. But it was the name of her father, so she called me Gigi. I go by my second name, 'Enzio.'"

Chapter 50

—

Ní neart go cur le chéile.
There is no strength without unity.

—Irish Proverb

The whole story came pouring out of him. He and Nicola met in the prison and worked the vineyard together. Nicola bragged about inheriting a vast vineyard in the near future. He coached Enzio to get the job as manager, and if he did, they would partner together to manage the rest of the 'difficulties' in the way of his inheritance.

"The first difficulty was to create a new will and get Marcella to sign it. That was when I learned Nicola was far from being the inheritor of the estate. But I was already tied up with his plans and we moved forward. Nicola was slowly adding to her medications, a drug he'd obtained to cause mental confusion. When she was sufficiently *confuso,* the plan was that I would slip the document in with other invoices and bills for her signature."

He wiped his face with a handkerchief and continued, "On that day, though she signed the papers, she expressed concern about some bills she hadn't authorized. These were bills Nicola had padded to pay for some of his own gambling debts. I couldn't show these to her, but to stall, I asked her to accompany me to the office. She was in front of me; she must have gotten dizzy from too much *medicinali*, or she blacked out. I don't know! She fell. I knew right away I could not help her. *Dio mio!* What have we done?"

"Are you willing to make things right? Will you tell your story to *la polizia?*" Giulio said.

"I cannot go back there! But I didn't kill anyone. What can I do?"

"You can testify, and hope things go easy by coming forward. We must call *la polizia*, but I don't want to scare off Nicola. Shall we all go together to the big house and talk to him?"

"What is this? Is something wrong? I thought you three were headed to Firenze by now." Nicola opened the door to them and invited the party into the library. "And why is Enzio here?"

"There is a little problem we need to discuss with you," Giulio said. "Sit down, brother. This may take a while."

Nicola sat. "Now I am worried. What is it?"

"It is the little matter of you and Enzio conspiring to drug mamma and have her sign a new will by fraud."

Nicola jumped up. "Enzio! What have you done?"

"They already knew! *They* told *me* what we did!"

"*Impossibile!*"

"Settle down, Nicola. It's not like we are accusing you of murdering mamma, though please tell me that was not the next step of your plan once you had the new will. Mamma's accident was no accident though, if you count the drugged state she was in when she fell, no thanks to you."

"You can't prove this," Nicola smouldered.

"Enzio has already agreed to testify against you. *La polizia* are on the way. I just wanted to hear if from you first."

"It's not what you think. I was cheated out of my inheritance. I am the firstborn; the estate should have gone to me. I was just righting what was wrong," Nicola fumed.

"You disappeared. If we had known you were in

prison, we could have helped you, visited you. You know mamma would have brought you her biscotti, *per l'amor del cielo*. Mamma did try to find you. You know this. You paid off her investigator. But he, too, like Enzio, has had a change of heart, a tugging of his conscience. Now it is your turn. You're still my brother. *Ti voglio bene, fratello.* If you resolve this, I am willing to share the business as well as the estate with you — fifty-fifty."

Deirdre and Moira stared at Giulio, amazed at the bigness of his heart and his offer to this treacherous brother.

"What do you mean by 'resolve this?'" Nicola asked, suspicion in his voice.

"I fear that if we bring forth mamma's original will, there will be severe repercussions for you as well as Enzio. I will not press charges against the medicine-tampering. It won't bring mamma back. Enzio doesn't need to be involved, though I believe we should hire a new manager."

Turning to Enzio, he said, "I will give you notice of one month to look for a new position and I will provide you with references. But I will be watching, and if I hear that you are involved in any similar schemes as this, I will come forth with evidence against you."

"That is more than I can expect, *signore*. *Grazie*."

Turning back to Nicola, he said, "There is just the matter of the drugs given to mamma. What did you give her to cause her to be so foggy that she signed that will?"

"No drugs! I would never do that! It was merely an herbal sleep aid. Tony's wife gave it to me. She said it would help her sleep, that is all!"

"What exactly were the herbs?" Deirdre asked.

"She told me it was Valerian and Kava Kava."

"Separately each is very good for helping with anxiety and restful sleep, but when combined, the results are dizziness, confusion, and impaired judgment. Loss of motor control is also likely and would explain Marcella's fall on the stairs as well as her unknowingly signing the will," Deirdre said.

"Then her death *is* my fault!" Nicola said, burying his face in his hands.

"It is done. Nothing will bring her back. We will go down to the courthouse, and you will sign a deed giving over one half of the estate to me. We will be equal partners in the business and the inheritance."

"Why are you doing this? I would not do the same for you if the situation was reversed," Nicola said.

"You have not seen, heard and witnessed what I have over the past few days. I know now that the grave is not the end. Mamma is still with us, helping us. We are *una famiglia* not just for this life but in the next as well. Those relationships are, or should be, what this life is all about. We can build something *meravigliosa* here at *Vigna Mancuso*. I am willing to look into the *agriturismo* business if you are so keen on it, but I want to vet any potential investors. I don't trust your Frank and Tony."

Nicola laughed. "You are probably right about that, *fratellino. Bene, grazie.* But … you said *la polizia* were coming. They should be here by now."

"*Una piccola bugia bianca* on my part. We will go down to the courthouse together today and resolve the matter of the fraudulent will with this new agreement between us. *Bene?*"

"*Bene.* But what about your reservations for the Uffizi?"

"Another small fib. The reservations are for *domani.*"

"I can see this *bugia* is a problem for you, something you should try to overcome, *fratellino,*" Nicola said with a smile.

"*Sì.* We all have our faults."

Chapter 51

Is glas iad na cnoic i bhfad uainn
Faraway hills are green.

—Irish Proverb

The following day, Nicola joined the threesome for their outing to Firenze. The deed had been written and recorded at the courthouse, clearing the air between the two brothers and going a long way towards mending their fractured relationship. Over espressos overlooking the Piazza di San Giovanni, Nicola seemed deep in thought.

"What is on your mind, Nicola? You seem troubled by something," Giulio asked.

"I can't stop thinking about something you said yesterday. Things you have seen, heard and witnessed. What did you mean?"

"Ah. I am not sure I am at liberty to say. I must defer

to Moira, if she cares to elaborate." He looked at Moira and raised an eyebrow.

"Let me ask you this, Nicola. What do you believe happens to us when we die?" Moira began.

"Well, we go to heaven, of course. Or hell, if we've been truly bad and unrepentant," He replied.

"And where do you suppose that heaven is located?"

"A very good question, *bella* Moira. I don't know that I have ever given it much thought. I suppose, up in the sky?"

"And if I were to tell you that the spirit world is all around us, here on earth?" Moira asked.

"You mean, like ghosts are everywhere?" Nicola looked puzzled.

"Well, I prefer to call them spirits, but yes, when we die, our spirit separates from our body. The body lies in the ground —"

"Until the resurrection! Correct?" Giulio added.

"Until the resurrection," Moira continued. "And the spirit enters another dimension we call the Otherside. It's also called the spirit world, or the afterlife by some."

"And that is nearby?"

"It is very nearby. *Most* people can't see the spirits that reside on the Otherside …"

"Go on. I'm getting the feeling that you are about to share that *some* people *can* see these others …"

"*Sì.*"

"And you are one of them?"

"*Sì.*"

No one spoke for a while. Then Nicola began, "You have seen mamma?"

"I have seen her and spoken with her."

"*Bella* Moira, I knew you were special … What did she say about me?"

"She was very happy that you had returned. She was glad that Giulio had his brother back to be a companion, a support and friend. She missed you terribly when you were gone but loves you still very much."

Nicola took out a handkerchief and wiped his nose and eyes. "Allergies …" he said, apologetically.

Giulio laughed. "You have never had allergies! You are feeling the same as I when I sat in the room in Dublin and watched as Moira visited with mamma. Isn't it *fantastico?* Can you see how important it is to build strong family relationships? Life goes on! *La famiglia continua!*"

"It's overwhelming. It's one thing to be taught about a belief in heaven in *catechismo;* it is quite another to be talking with someone who has insider information."

No one spoke for a few moments, then Deirdre suggested, "Shall we continue our walk around this magnificent city?"

As they explored Florence, Giulio managed to manoeuvre Deirdre in front of their party, leaving Nicola and Moira to walk a few paces behind them.

"Moira has said she is ready to head back to Dublin soon, but I noticed you didn't respond that you also were ready to leave our *bella Italia* …"

"It would be hard to leave. It's a beautiful place, and I feel there is a lot more I'd like to explore."

"Is that all that is keeping you from wanting to leave?"

She took his hand and gave it a squeeze. "You know it's not. It would be a big step for me to stay here with you, though. And technically, you haven't asked me …"

He stopped in the middle of the sidewalk and took both her hands in his. "*Amo, ti adoro!* Will you stay with me, at least for longer? I don't ask you to make a permanent commitment right now. Let us get used to the idea of being together, a couple once again; even more so than we were in Ireland. If you cannot make Italy your home, I will return to your home with you."

"Let me think on it a bit longer? I promise I will give you an answer this evening."

"*Arrivederci, bella* Moira! Come back to us anytime! I will be your personal tour guide to *bella Italia!*" Nicola said, kissing Moira's cheeks and handing over her suitcase he had carried into the airport from the car.

Giulio stepped forward and hugged Moira. "Thank you again for all you've done for me, for us. You have brought us together and given us peace and healing."

Deirdre hugged her sister tight for more than a moment, whispering in her ear, *"Tell me I'm doing the right thing …"*

"You are following your heart. You will be grand, and I will be grand. And if you are still here in a few months, I will be back with Nuala for a visit. And maybe even bring Ma along!"

"Thank you. But you may be too busy contacting that long list of Magdalenes now that you'll be working with the JFMs."

Moira pulled apart from the embrace, kissed her sister on both cheeks and said, "Slán a fhágáil agat agus tú a fheiceáil go luath."

"See you soon …" Deirdre echoed.

AUTHOR'S NOTE:

—

Gone But Not Forgotten is based on a true story from my Canadian ancestry. My great-great-grandparents emigrated from Quebec to the United State in 1879 with their eight children, leaving the ninth and youngest, Amanda, age three, with a neighbour. It was fifty years before Amanda was finally reunited with two of her remaining siblings. You can find the whole story here: https://gailgrantpark. com/siblings-reunited-after-decades-apart/

The Magdalene Laundries, Mother and Baby Homes and Industrial Schools of Ireland that I've written about in *Buried Secrets* were real institutions that were exposed for their cruelties and inhumane treatment of their inmates in 1993 when a laundry property was sold, and a mass grave of unnamed women was discovered. The *Justice For Magdalenes* (JFM) organization did present at the United Nations and petitioned the Irish government for redress for victims. The names of all the participants and specific locations have been changed in this fictionized account.

Resources for further information:

1. Blakemore, Erin. "How Ireland Turned 'Fallen Women' into slaves." Updated: July 21, 2019, Original: March 12, 2018 https://www.history.com/news/magdalene-laundry-ireland-asylum-abuse

2. Matthews, Dylan. "How Mid-Century Ireland dealt with unwed mothers and their children". Vox Media LLC, 5 June 2014, https://www.vox.com/2014/6/5/5779902/how-mid-century-ireland-dealt-with-unwed-mothers-and-their-children

3. Ostberg, René. "Magdalene laundry". *Encyclopaedia Britannica*, 21 Nov. 2023, https://www.britannica.com/topic/Magdalene-laundry Accessed 21 October 2024

RECIPES

Cén t-im agus an t-uisce beatha nach leigheasfaidh, níl aon leigheas air.
What butter and whiskey won't cure, there is no cure for.

—Irish saying

POTATO FARLS

——

Ingredients:

    3 medium to large potatoes, peeled
    1 big dollop of butter (about 60 grams)
    120g flour plus extra for dusting (1 cup)
    ¾ tsp baking powder
    ½ tsp salt

Instructions:

1. First boil the potatoes for 20-25 mins so they are super soft. Mash them with the butter and allow to cool

2. Add in the flour, baking powder and salt and mix to a dough

3. Add to a floured surface, roll out to ¼" thickness and cut into squares

4. Fry on a dry pan for 4-5 minutes on each side. If serving as part of a fry up fry in oil for an additional 1-2 mins on each side.

5. Serve with butter or jam spread on top.

Nuala's Sweet Apple Bread

———

Ingredients:

    250g (cups) white flour
    1 tsp baking soda
    ½ tsp salt
    60g (1/2 cup) salted butter
    2 tart apples (Bramley or Granny Smith, peeled and grated)
    125g (cup) Golden Caster Sugar
    1/2 tsp vanilla bean paste
    2 eggs, beaten
    2 tsp evaporated milk
    1 cup raisins and nuts, optional

Instructions:

1. Sift together dry ingredients. Cream together butter and sugar

2. Stir in beaten eggs one at a time. Combine with dry ingredients.

3. Add grated apple, milk and vanilla paste. Beat until smooth. Add optional ingredients

4. Pour into greased bread pan. Mix 3 Tablespoons of sugar with 1 tsp cinnamon, spread evenly over top of bread. Bake @ 350 for 1 hour until golden brown. Insert toothpick to test.

VANILLA BEAN PASTE RECIPE

——

Ingredients:
Vanilla beans – 5-6 cut into small pieces
113g (½ cup) sugar
118ml (½ cup) water

Instructions:

In a blender, mix sugar and vanilla beans. Powder it finely. Combine powdered mixture and water in saucepan, mix well. Bring it to a boil and simmer for 5 mins. Remove it from heat and let it cool. Blend again to a fine puree. Cool this mixture completely. Store in clean glass jar in refrigerator for up to three months.

IRISH APPLE CAKE

———

Ingredients for Cake:
- 360g (3&2/3 cups) cake flour
- 110g/ (cup) cane sugar
- 2 teaspoons baking powder
- 1/2 teaspoon salt
- 1/4 teaspoon nutmeg
- 1/8 teaspoon cloves
- 100g (1/2 cup) salted butter, melted and cooled
- 70 ml (1/4) cup oil
- 2 large eggs
- 22 ml (3/4 cup) whole milk
- 1 teaspoon pure vanilla extract
- 4 Bramley or Granny Smith apples (tart!), peeled and diced
- 2 Tablespoons cane sugar, to sprinkle over top of cake

Instructions for the Cake:

1. Preheat oven to 185°C/375°F. Spray a 9-inch springform pan with cooking spray and set aside.

2. In a large bowl, whisk together cake flour, sugar, baking powder, salt, cloves and nutmeg.

3. In a separate bowl, whisk together the melted butter, oil, eggs, milk, and vanilla.

4. Peel and core apples, slicing into bite-size chunks, then

add to the flour mixture, tossing to combine.

5. Add the milk mixture to the flour and apples mixture, stirring just until combined to create a sticky dough. Transfer to the prepared pan, spreading to the edges and sprinkling with the extra sugar on top.

6. Bake for 45 to 50 minutes, or until a sharp knife stuck into the center of the cake comes out clean and the top is golden brown.

Ingredients for Custard Sauce
> 355ml (1&1/2 cup) whole milk
> 114g (1/2 cup) cane sugar
> 6 large egg yolks
> 2 teaspoons pure vanilla extract

Instructions for Custard Sauce

1. Heat the milk in a heavy bottomed medium size saucepan over medium heat until bubbles begin to appear around the edges of the pan.

2. Meanwhile, whisk the sugar and egg yolks for 2-3 minutes, until the mixture is thickened slightly and pale yellow.

3. Slowly whisk half of the hot milk into the egg/ sugar mixture to temper the egg yolks. Then pour the tempered yolks back into the saucepan with the remaining milk and continue to cook and stir over medium heat until the custard begins to thicken slightly,

about 3-4 minutes. It should be thick enough to coat the back of a spoon.

4. Remove custard sauce from heat and stir in the vanilla or vanilla bean paste. Serve warm or cold over Irish apple cake. The custard sauce will keep for up to 1 week in the refrigerator.

NUALA'S STICKY PRUNE AND DATE CAKE

For the glaze:
    1½ tablespoons orange marmalade
    ½ tablespoon water

For the cake:
    175g (6 oz) dates, stoned and chopped
    125g (4 oz) prunes, chopped
    75g (3 oz) raisins
    75g (3oz) currants
    200g (7 oz) salted butter
    200ml (6.7 oz) water
    300g (10 oz) sweetened condensed milk
    110g (cup) white flour
    110g (cup) whole wheat flour
    pinch of salt
    ½ level teaspoon baking soda
    1 rounded tablespoon orange marmalade

Instructions:

1. Preheat oven to 170°C/325°F

2. Combine fruits, butter, water and condensed milk in a saucepan. Bring to boil, stirring frequently to prevent it sticking.

3. Reduce heat and simmer for 3 minutes– still stirring occasionally.

4. Transfer mixture to a large mixing bowl; let cool for 30 minutes.

5. While it's cooling, sift together flours, salt and bicarbonate of soda. Add in any bran left in the sieve from the whole wheat. When the fruit mixture has cooled, stir in the dry ingredients, plus the tablespoon of marmalade.

6. Spoon mixture into baking tin that has been lined with parchment. Level it off with the back of a tablespoon. Bake on a lower shelf for 1 hour and 50 minutes. Check halfway through, if top is browning to quickly, cover with foil or baking parchment. Let cake cool in tin for 5 minutes before turning it out to cool on a wire tray.

7. When the cake is completely cold, gently heat the marmalade in a small saucepan with the water. Brush over the top of the cake. Store in an airtight container.

DEIRDRE'S BUBBLE AND SQUEAK

Ingredients:

6 tablespoons unsalted butter, or vegetable oil
1/2 cup finely chopped onion
1 pound mashed potatoes, about 2 cups
1 cup leftover vegetables (cabbage, kale, peas, cooked swede, cooked carrots, and/or cooked Brussels sprouts), finely chopped
Bacon, leftover roast, bangers, and/or ham, chopped, optional
Salt, to taste
Freshly ground black pepper, to taste
Fried or poached eggs, for serving, optional

Instructions:

1. Fry chopped onions in butter until soft.

2. Add mashed potatoes, leftover meat and vegetables. Cook and stir for about 10 minutes until heated through.

3. Press the mixture into the base of the pan and let cook for one minute. Turn over, press and cook for another minute until both sides are slightly browned.

NANA BRIGID'S BREAD AND BUTTER PUDDING

---

1. Butter several slices of stale bread and layer into a baking tin.
2. Sprinkle raisins and sugar between the layers
3. Sprinkle nutmeg on top
4. Whisk two to four eggs, depending on tin size, into enough milk to completely cover the bread mixture and it has absorbed the milk. Leave room in the tin for it to rise and cook in a heated oven until browned.
5. 180°C/350°F for 30-40 minutes until browned and a knife comes out clean.

MOLLY'S COLCANNON

———

Ingredients (serves 24):
    9 pounds baking potatoes peeled & quartered
    1½ cup cream, warmed
    ¾ cup butter melted, more as needed
    2 white onion or 4 leeks
    2 heads cabbage (approx. 15 cups)
    9 tablespoons butter melted

Instructions:

1. Bring a large pot of salted water to a boil. Add the potatoes and simmer for 12-15 minutes or until fork tender.

2. While the potatoes are cooking, prepare the onions or leeks, and cabbage. Dice the white onion into ½-inch pieces or slice the white and light green parts of the leeks thinly and rinse well. Cut the cabbage into 1-inch pieces.

3. Melt butter in a large skillet over medium heat. Cook the onion or leeks and cabbage in the butter until the onion is translucent and the cabbage is tender.

4. Once the potatoes are cooked, drain them and return them to the warm pot. Mash the potatoes with a potato masher, adding cream and butter as needed to reach

a smooth consistency. Season with salt and pepper.

5. Gently fold the mashed potatoes, cabbage, and onions together.

Transcript of BYU-I (Brigham Young University-Idaho) Radio interview with the author, November 27, 2023

BYU-I: Let's talk about this first book. How long did it take you to write it, and when did it debut?

Gail Grant Park: Probably, from start to finish a little over two years from the idea then to the launch on October 23, 2023. It was a long process. The writing part went fairly quickly. I had a shorter version, but then I sent it to an editor, and he said it was too short and a bit disjointed; more like a collection of short stories and I needed to add another story that would tie them all together. So, I went back to the writing desk and wrote a fourth story that tied them all together. Then there were edits and rewrites. Getting the cover done also took some time.

BYU-I: I feel like that's fairly quick!

Gail: I thought it was. I sent it to several small publishing houses and got one response from a publisher who was interested, but said they liked to do series and expected their authors to do 2-3 books a year. I *might* be able to do a second book in a year, but I don't know how authors can do 2-3 in a year.

BYU-I: Let's talk about the premise of your book. What's the main issue to be solved?

Gail: It's grown as I've started writing book two. There's a little bit of me in each of the three sisters. I have Irish ancestry; one of the Gallagher Girls' grandmothers is a Connolly, and their other grandmother is an O'Brien; both names come from my family tree. I have cousins also living in Ireland now — third cousins once removed I believe is the connection there. I went to Ireland with my daughter this past year and finally met several of those cousins. They helped me quite a bit with names, pronunciations, the slang and geographical locations.

With my Irish ancestry and love of all things Irish, I felt compelled to put the setting there. I know it's a bit presumptuous of me to write about a culture not my own, but when my cousins read the book, they said I'd done a pretty good job.

I'd say the premise is that the veil is thin between this world and the spirit world, and our ancestors are there watching over us. Moira's deceased grandmother is her guardian angel, watching over her.

BYU-I: You said you felt parallels to your own life besides just being Irish. Would you talk about that?

Gail: Sure. In one part of the book, Moira is driving at night and falls asleep at the wheel. The spirit of her deceased friend Julia calls out to her, "Wake up, Moira! You're going to crash!" and she wakes up in time to stop the car from hitting the bridge. That happened to my cousin who was going through a bad situation. She was up late at night driving to get away from an abusive spouse. She fell asleep at the wheel and was awakened by her deceased sister's voice telling her to wake up, she's going to crash. She was able to steer away from the guardrail and avoid an accident.

Little things like that. There's another scene in the beginning when Moira is confronted with a menacing spirit that binds her tongue, preventing her from calling out for help. Latter-day Saint readers will recognize that as a part of Joseph Smith's experience during his First Vision.

I wanted to give a glimpse of the spirit world as it really is. There are so many ghost stories out there that aren't real…well, this one isn't *real* either, but it is my belief as a member of the Church of Jesus Christ of Latter-day Saints of what the spirit world is like and what happens there. There is a fine line between this world and the next and the spirits of our loved ones who've departed are watching over us.

My neighbor read the book and stopped me on the street the other day and said, "Okay, now is this a story about you and your life, is this a true story?" I replied that some of the instances sorta-kinda happened to people I know. He said, "I knew it! I knew that it must be a story of you and your grandmother who was helping you. I feel like my deceased grandmother has been watching over me and helping me for years."

I feel like that belief really resonates with people and they can identify with that.

BYU-I: I love that! I love the preserved kinship through the veil aspect which is pretty cool.

So, what can people hope for in books to come? Are they about these same characters?

Gail: The three sisters carry on in each book. There's an arc developing for Moira. She's had some negative publicity. They've solved several cases working with the local gardaí/police, and there's a newspaper man who pooh-poohed them saying, "they aren't real detectives — girls can't be real detectives." (Which actually happened to me, but I'll talk about that later). Therefore, Moira has this chip on her shoulder that she has to prove she's a real detective. She's smart and can solve the mysteries without being told everything by the spirits. So, her grandmother takes a step back and lets her spread her wings, gives her an opportunity to develop her skills to show she's a real detective. The story shows her honing her talents but also recognizing that her talent and gift really is her communication with the departed and she needs to honor and appreciate that and not think she is any less of a detective for relying on the spirits to guide her.

BYU-I: Do you want to share what happened to you that was similar?

Gail: Well, when I was a young girl, aged 9-10, I loved reading Nancy Drew and Trixie Belden mysteries. I devoured them! I wanted to be a detective, so my friend and I started a detective agency we called Instant Investigations. We made business cards and rode our bikes around town solving (nonexistent) crimes. There were a couple boys in our class that said, "Girls can't be real detectives, only boys are detectives." I was crushed! I couldn't say, well Nancy and Trixie are detectives and they're girls, because I knew they were fictional characters. I was so deflated. I came home devasted. My dad — bless his heart, noticed I was not happy and got the story out of me. He said, "Don't you pay any attention to those boys, they have no idea. You can be anything you want to be."

That support was huge. I went on to be a detective. I joined the Church of Jesus Christ of Latter-day Saints and found out about the importance of genealogy and family history work, and I became a detective of missing persons, discovering my ancestors. There's nothing better than solving family history mysteries. So I had to have Moira go through that struggle to know what she was doing was legitimate and worthwhile.

BYU-I: Absolutely. That's wonderful. Those really are the mysteries that have impact for eternity. I think that's wonderful that you channeled that desire into your own genealogy and now you are showing readers the excitement of that.

Gail: I hope it will appeal on a lot of different levels. There's the ancestry thing, the guardian angel thing and the Irish thing. A little bit of something for everyone.

BYU-I: Absolutely. Great! Is there anything you'd like to tell your readers as to why they should read your book?

Gail: Well, it's written from the heart. I put my heart and soul into it. I go around all day with these three women with me. Everything I see reminds me of them. I see a Mini Cooper and say, "There's Moira's car!"

They have become real to me, and I hope they are endearing enough that they will become real to them.

BYU-I: Is there anything else you'd like to share?

Gail: There's a little bit of me in each of the sisters. The part of Deirdre that is me is that I'm also an herbalist as she is. All her herbal knowledge comes from what I have studied in herbal medicine. Nuala is a dreamer, and I also dabble in dream work. I'm in groups that share dreams and try to discern their inner meaning. And Moira is the detective. She and I share one little fault, which hopefully is not that obvious, but we don't like small talk. If I have something to say to someone, I'll pick up the phone and say, "Do you have such and such I can borrow?" I can't say, "so, how are you? How's your day going?" And that's me in Moira. We just get right down to business.

BYU-I: You cut to the chase.

Gail: Exactly.

BYU-I: and where can readers find you?

Gail: I'm on Facebook, Instagram and my website is gailgrantpark.com.

BYU-I: Thank you for speaking with us today.

Gail: Thank you for having me!

Also by Gail Grant Park

The Gallagher Girls Mystery Series
We Are Shadows: An Irish Ghost Story
The Body in Brú na Bóinne

"Escape in Three Movements" in the anthology,
Rainfall: A Rainy Day Writers Anthology

About the Author

Gail Grant Park is the author of *We Are Shadows: An Irish Ghost Story*, the first novel in the Gallagher Girls Mystery series. Gail holds a BA in history from Brigham Young University and an MLIS from Syracuse University. A librarian, genealogist and herbalist, Gail now writes and creates art from her home in Boise, Idaho.

The Body in Brú na Bóinne is the second in the Gallagher Girls Mystery series, followed by *A Haunting at Hawthorn*.

You can find Gail at:
https://gailgrantpark.com
www.facebook.com/ParkCreativewriting/

9 798991 967907